GHOULISH GAMES
TURN TO STONE FOR 3 ROLLS!
MOVE 5 SPACES
HOWL AT THE MOON
BACK TO START!
HAIL SATAN!
GAME OVER!
FOOD
GAME OVER!
KEEP OUT
MEET THE WHITE LADY !!!
MOVE TO SQUARE BELOW
UFO ABDUCTION!
LUCKY YOU!!!
MOVE 7 SPACES
KISS A WITCH LOSE A TURN!
BACK TO START!
ROLL DIE!
SEAL YOUR FATE?!
DO NOT ENTER
KICK A PUMPKIN
MOVE 4 SPACES...
ROLL A DIE!!!
START!
SPEND THE NIGHT IN A GRAVEYARD!
MOVE 3 SPACES
BAD LUCK
BACK 2 SPACES
BLOOD DONATION
BACK TO START!

Venture
Illustrated©

Mystic Boxing Commission
Los Angeles, CA

Opposite page: "Ghoulish Games" by Fitz.
Frontispiece (far front) artwork by Edd Cartier

Venture Illustrated©

Published by:

Publisher/Editor/Designer: Daniel Yaryan

MBC Artist: Mat Fitzsimmons
Front Cover Artist: Lawrence Sterne Stevens
Back Cover Artist: Ara Azul

Contributing Creatives:
Johannes Josephus Aarts, Rudolf Bauer
Max Beckmann, Paul Behrens, Hannes Bok
Edd Cartier, Richard V. Correll, Ed Emshwiller
Michael C Ford, James Gabriel, Jerry Kamstra
Wassily Kandinsky, Ernst Ludwig Kirchner
H.P. Lovecraft, Ellyn Maybe, Paul Orban
Andrew Orillion, Frank R. Paul, Barye Phillips
Ruben Quintana, Odilon Redon, Jery V. Stier
L.R. Summers, Pamela Swift, Lyn Venable
T. Mike Walker, Karl Wiener, Hannah Yaryan

ISBN#: 979-8-9930896-1-4
Issue #1, 1st Edition
December 2025—Mystic Boxing Commission

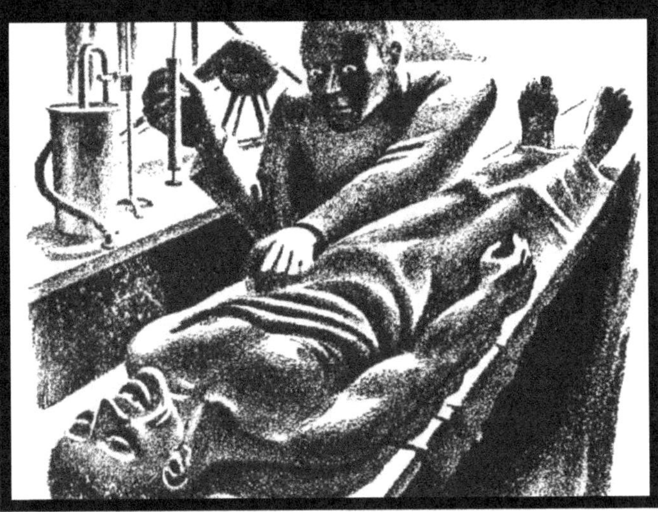

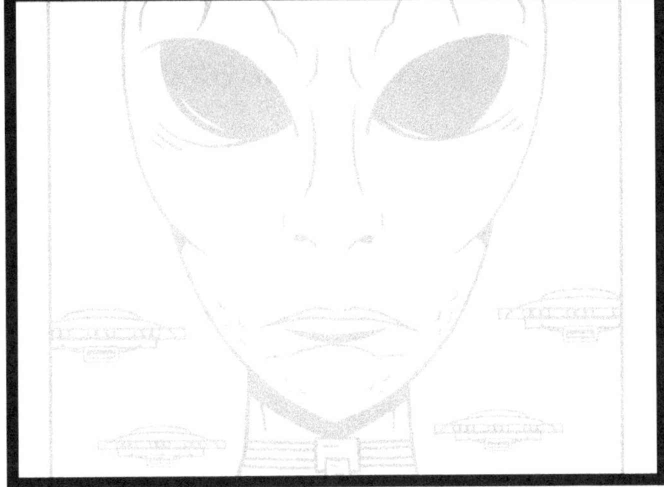

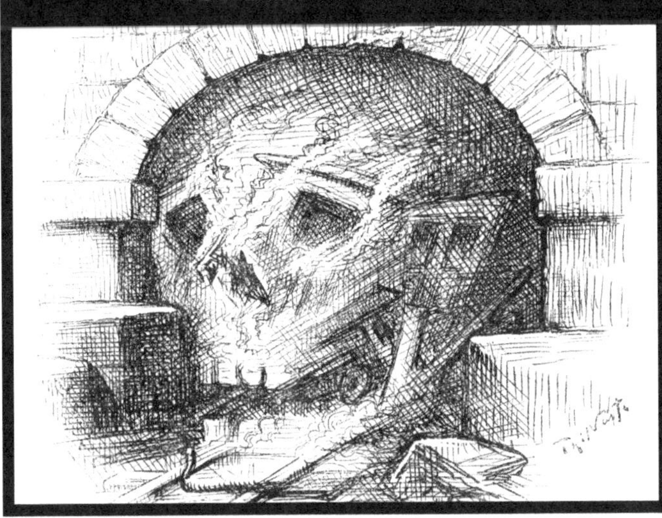

exp. date: 10/10/2059
HAVE YOU SEEN ME?
Name: Jay Smith
D.O.B. 10/10/10
Last Seen on: 07/08/2019
Montauk, NY
Please Call:
G-ONE-MIS-SING
4-663-647-7464
FARMS
MILK
1/2 gallon

WHO TURN MEN TAMELY

By Michael C Ford

The strong-minded women
Who turn men tamely
Without a doubt
Are a dangerous lot

-Desmond O'Grady

They wore synthetic aluminum jumpsuits flattering to variously feminine attractiveness. But just as varied were the levels at which they were stationed as members of the Interrogation Squad. One level of female activators were, simultaneously, flipping crescent moon-shaped toggle switches motivating enormous reel-to-reel recording tapes.

Designated on another level was a location where women were operating huge, computerized receivers which helped to, accordingly, assimilate and document the last words of the last male politician on Earth.

With quality, with formality, with conviction and a profound commitment to her assignment, a former cinema actress with the unlikely name of Vanilla Venus still being recognized as some former derelict ingénue in films bi-weekly screened and celebrated at the Intergalactic Entertainment Center & Dream Dome; also, (as irony would have it) once portrayed a seductive secretary in the 2155 Stratusphunk Film Company production of *Midnight In a Madhouse*. She's now seen crossing her professional legs, beginning her task of taking shorthand notes on a loose-leaf pad, in a workspace very near to where the city of Pittsburgh was, at one time in the 21st Century, located, while, outside, blowing off what used to be the Monongahela: now known as Big Mama Thornton River with 1950's Rhythm & Blues retro-riverboat cruises, a brisk draft whistled and wailed across a nuclear-blasted wasteland caused by the Armageddon Wars of 2095. All this vacancy was creating a totally flattened and barren landscape all the way through un-populated roadways leading into Washington, D.C.

Wild winds nipped at the bare branches of walnut trees planted there long ago, supplying shade, before the invention of mechanical sunlight made that luxury obsolete. When shade was needed for any reason of choice or necessity, they just turned off the sun.

This storm was a particularly unstoppable one roistering all the way to where it was braced by chunks of concrete, formerly known as the infamous Watergate Hotel: but it had been, eventually, turned into a feminist lesbian singles bistro nostalgically named Nixon's Mill House.

There was an absence of occupants in the no-longer used grandstands. What few officials there temporarily gathered, in solemn clumps of human shrapnel around a bleached portico, were from an organization conceived as Consciousness Underworld of Neoteric Termination: otherwise initialized as C.U.N.T: Some were standing under giant loudspeakers and balanced

CONTINUED, NEXT PAGE...

Artwork by T Mike Walker

...CONTINUED, FROM LAST PAGE

by spare branches of autumn's skeletal trees.

Apparently, not too many members of the Female Auxiliary were particularly eager to hear the last words of this last political pundit. All-together, they appeared to be more inclined to dismiss the world arena of contemporary politics, so dominant, during the last few generations of a non-existent Congress and Senate and, quite obviously, in the process of eliminating more useless throwaway authority figures who went the way of the stagecoach, the Studebaker auto and the locomotive. They went the way of the idealistic knight-in-shiny-sharkskin private eye, the leering burlesque comic, the black and white movie, the blue-collar criminal, the two-tone

"The dying voice of the Last Politician began in a reedy quavering tenor: Admittedly, standing, always, upon dreadfully insecure turf, moving around never meant anything to me."

chrome dream cars and the girls who slid behind computerized wheels–exposing their driving-men-crazy predilections.

Coincidentally, entombment for this final male occupant of the White House oval office had been prepared right here, in D.C. at The Library of Congress having been long ago renamed The Best Cellar Library Mausoleum. His marker is a mottled slab. And engraved (if you'll forgive the outrageous, albeit unwarranted pun) with just two simply carved words insultingly directed at one of his most popular political characteristics: HERE LIES.

The dying voice of the Last Politician began in a reedy quavering tenor: *Admittedly, standing, always, upon dreadfully insecure turf, moving around never meant anything to me.*

The man who'd been appointed Director of the Federation Media Control Unit had, several years before, been master of ceremonies at the Church of The Hydrogen Virgin. This was a neo-religious project located in the Northern section of Idaho, at the confluence of the Clearwater and the Snake Rivers.

Only a few years ago, that location had been renamed The Joan Rivers; and was now being used

CONTINUED, NEXT PAGE...

Artwork by T Mike Walker

...CONTINUED, FROM LAST PAGE

as an annual outdoor festival for a brigandage of female comics doing summer vacation shtick for, otherwise, unwary reveling travelers.

The gentleman, with the title DIRECTOR stenciled on a plastic tag pinned to his thin brown Oxford-cloth overcoat, was picking at the badge like it was a wart. Then, he started waving his right arm in the air, as though it were an ancient energy conservation pamphlet found in an attic full of Democratic and GOP crud.

"After all," he said, "that government puppet has been dumped or, literarily, will be bounced-out of business." He was waving both arms, by now, seemingly, as an indication that his original outburst had been nauseatingly inspired by some deeper hysteria. "Y'know," he continued, "I can't hardly figure any strict necessity, y'see, for you to put squiggles in a shorthand book, when there are, already, six-hundred and sixty hours of ludicrously recorded boredom." He was staring at the Acting Secretary's skirt riding up some delicately contoured silk.

Completely aware of his lascivious gaze, the Acting Secretary readjusted her position offering him a more available view. Her writing utensil continued to wriggle on the page, it seemed somehow, independently.

The recorded voice strengthened to a wimpy drone. *It has been my last wish to speak to you all, in a way, not unlike the manner in which I addressed the Cosmopolitan Loyalists, as if I was conducting hymns on a sinking cruise yacht. Now, damnitall, to the Devil...that's what I call politics.*

Meanwhile, the Director stood in back of the Secretary's chair, where he could more easily browse in the vicinity of her décolletage which puckered like an awning in a hot wind.

About nine hours into these final recorded words, the Director decided that this whole thing, too, had been reminding him of all those dull, dim-witted lectures in the big auditorium. "You remember, don't you Madam Secretary, the drinking and the carousing and the cursing and the left-wing liberal level of plebian resentment in the halls of academe?"

The recorded politician's voice went on: *...as if talking about women were, indeed, sincere and truly objective: that is in the truly subjective sense, well, hell, then. . . just talking to them should be equally egalitarian. Gosh darn it. And, by Heaven, that's what I call EQUALITY! Understand, my Fellow constituents, it will be WIVES who, sometimes, dear ones be though they may, will wish to create rather bizarre tangents, too, and I'm going to use a big word here TAME. . . yes, tame even the most flexible boss...I do mean to say... ergo...dispensable husband...*

The Director's hands, like two aggressive leeches, clutched at the Acting Secretary's shoulders. "I've always been somewhat flexible myself," he said.

. . .even to the point where some family spouse becomes a bandage covering a behemoth wound—the unctuous voice oozed on—we see how sinister family life has evolved beneath the wound; as it might very well be, either abusive or indifferent wives with not much to define them, except genial resignation, pasteurized emotions and transforming into aimless energy drains.

The sultry Acting Secretary shrugged off the invasive hands of the Director the way a sharp breeze might invite a flock of seagulls to abandon the weathered roof of a beach-front motel.

The Director swiveled himself around to face her full-on and dropping to his knees like a penitent, he offered familiar utterance of the stand-up comic phrase: "Take my wife. . .please!"

The girl quit wriggling her Ticonderoga pencil, looking down at the man through aquamarine slits and asking: "Ah, you are a patriot of the ancient comedians, my dear Director?"

"It's just that you remind me so much," he answered, "of my darling mistress. She was such a gossamer example as I recall."

CONTINUED, NEXT PAGE...

The girl was leaning slowly, sensually, backwards and provocatively chewing her eraser.

The man who wore the Director's name tag intoned: "So, then as she was revealed to my wife; quite by some sloppy, serendipitous mix-up in plans, to be sure, my sweet compassionate mistress. . .well. . was disappeared. . . not unlike vaporization symbols in a chemistry notebook. My marriage, alas, had been saved!"

The oily voice of the last male politician on Earth crooned on in an indefatigable manner, not to mention, into the coincidentally eleventh hour. *I think it's going to be increasingly necessary for everyone to have cognition of the fact that thinking is synonymous with. . . oh, no, I guess I don't know...homonyms...antonyms...*

The Director started, quite suddenly and quite violently, coughing. Pulling out a freshly laundered handkerchief, he stood up, awkwardly, looking like a human question mark, continued hacking and gagging and spraying guinea-pig pink splotches into his fresh white linen. When he finished his fit, he whined, as if it were a weird sort of duplicitous duet with the recorded voice; then puking out his own vile sentiments. "Oh, how I'd sit in cafeterias and cocktail bars and hotel rooms with my mistress. She always made me feel like a coarse piece of flannel she'd been, in her own tender fashion, revising...and turning into burnished cotton...

"The girl crossed her legs. again, with a silky lisp. Her feet were stacked in boots with animal-skin brocade. All of sudden, she allowed one of her conical toes to chuck the Director under his triple chins, pitching him over into an awkward heap."

oh, my yes...and, needing-ly; so, I, then would begin to imagine impossible revisions." Dropping to his knees, again, the Director, in a rather quaint, however, futile attempt to peek up the Acting Secretary's dress, continued babbling: "You must understand certain necessities exist, when a man's...ungh...urgencies, yes, urgencies become like emotional pressure cookers at the moment, when he's, suddenly, realizing his dear mistress...ungh, I mean wife, in the meantime, had been transformed

CONTINUED, NEXT PAGE...

...CONTINUED, FROM LAST PAGE

into a lukewarm TV dinner. I mean, you do, totally, understand. . . don't you, Madam sexretary. . .ungh. . . I mean. . .SECretary?"

The girl crossed her legs. again, with a silky lisp. Her feet were stacked in boots with animal-skin brocade. All of sudden, she allowed one of her conical toes to chuck the Director under his triple chins, pitching him over into an awkward heap. It was as if he were playing

"Now, the Director was cringing like a compromised masochist with a suddenly embarrassing aversion to punishment."

submissive for a dominant prostitute.

"The only thing I understand," she said, finally, in a voice that would have given a polar bear frostbite, "is that all of you weak, pompous, deluded dingo males with proclivity towards giving me erotic genuflections need some kind of manic erasure therapy of your own; and indeed, allowing inspiration for you to go into a Claude Rains imitation of *The Invisible Man*. I'm your audience, my dear Director...entertain me!"

The last male politician, as though interrupting himself through some weird emulation, in mid-sentence, coughed and spit-up a thick gorpy bile into a well-placed potted fern, apparently near enough to his microphone, after which, in a strangled delivery, he continued...*must learn to ride the horse of responsibility into the barn!*

Now, the Director was cringing like a compromised masochist with a suddenly embarrassing aversion to punishment. When he spoke, it was at piped decibels that resembled a kind of suffocated shriek. "Please. . .ungh. . .Ma'am. . .ungh, Miss. . .ungh, Ms. . .ergh, whatever. . .no one is more overjoyed than I myself to know that the time has finally arrived for a woman. . .*neé* all womankind…you must forgive me being so remiss. . .forgive my need for all of you to assume the roles, as rulers. You see, I do so truly wish to decipher the map to that long-lost goldmine found only in the moist hidden alcoves of your most private property I, always, enjoy referring to as Quim Valley."

The tape wheels unwound the final few moments in what had to be the last hour of the, by now, dead Last Politician, as was the spent voice of his recorded brain he had been, in his last years, lip-synching, and, at this amazing moment kept on stammering and, not to mention, just plain dying-out. *Now's the time I'm really and truly feeling it, as if I was. . .I mean as if most of. . .even the more subtle. . .ungh. . . nuances of democratic acquisition. . .had been . . like ballerinas in street drag. . .standing before. . .the big box-office. . .of eternity. . .where. . ungh. . .well. . .there are no. . .no more . . .significant intermission cigars for sale.*

The Director staggered to a chair, sat down, folding his hands the way he might have done, if he'd been a discouraged evangelist. He was, still, talking to the girl, but he was addressing the floor. "Listen, you may be a movie starlet of unimportant vintage to some people, but to me you're a fantasy showgirl archetypal benefit for a billion opening night jitters." The Director's eyes began to twitch with the intensity of a candidate for a laughing academy straightjacket. "I mean, I want to treat you to a bottle of perfume and a bottle of Strega. I want to buy you jangling earrings and sexy accessories. Oh, if you'd only let me, I would buy you flowers and drugs. . .anything you so desire."

The Acting Secretary had been examining her mouth in a chromium compact mirror. She spoke into the mirror. "Really, Mr. Director, sir, I am moved to say that you appear to have quite relieved yourself of what I'm sure you are, still, under the delusion of at some point coming to your piquant senses."

Now the Director was leaping around the room like a demented kangaroo. "Listen to that disgrace of a political puppet of crooked government manipulation. . . that God-awful voice saying those God-awful pathetic final unnecessary words. He's as tepid and dull dead as he was when alive. I mean, at least, all government control was, at one time, issued by offices of LIVING criminals. . .and, now. . ."

"Ah, yes, now, my wise and wicked Director," the Acting Secretary patronizingly stated, "you see, all control to the contrary would appear to be, presently, under the ruling entities of an elite cadre of feminine domination."

The closing spoken idiotic measures by our very last male leader were, coincidentally, dealing with the immanent and frightful realization that this significant taking-charge agenda had been initiated by women... "*whose care and responsibility must be under signi-*

CONTINUED, NEXT PAGE...

D-274

35c

WHO TURN MEN TAMELY

The world was a no man's land

MICHAEL C FORD

Complete & Unabridged

Artwork by Ed Emshwiller

...CONTINUED

fied and dignified careful manners with which they have assumed control. . . and we of political royalty believe truly that they will treat all remaining men as though they were the thoughtful and desirable tokens of. . .dead souls, like...well, myself, as a distinguished. . .ungh. . . perhaps, or is it. . .well. . .at all possible that. . .ungh. . .these. . .well, that is to say. . .words be. . . well. . .like dead leaves under a . . .well, maybe. . . tree. . .in a maybe meadow and. . .that we all would find solace. . . somewhere. . . in the. . .ungh . . way they. . .crackle. . .and then disintegrate. . . and wait for. . .for. . .for. . .the fireman."

"Alright," the Director argued, paying no attention to the tape loops, as they spun out, disengaging from their carriages. "So, it will be entirely agreed then that, of course, rid the world of politicians, yes, a darn good idea, boy-oh-boy, but, for gosh sakes, y'know, really. . .to kill all the men? Oh, no not to do that, really, no, but, hey wait, a sec, y'know, most of the men are. . .y'know . . .dead I guess. . .now, with the possible exception. . ."

". . .of. . .YOU. . .my dear, dear Director!

"Oh, you're very dear to me yourself. I think of you in so many ways other than simply a fantasy starlet from motion picture kingdoms…but think of the kingdom I could assist you in perpetuating. . . don't you see, if. . ."

Abruptly interrupting, the Acting Secretary popped her thumbs and the Interrogators shut off their machines.

" . .oh, but wait. . .wait. . .really, actually," the Director

whimpered, "you've no idea the effect you always had on my. . .ah. . .ah. . .ah. . . I mean you must know. . .know that. . .making me realize how much of a source of revelation women of your social position. . ."

The women in aluminum jumpsuits put microphones back into their holsters. They shuttled from behind their glass booth encasements and surrounded the Director.

The Director's eyes flashed like a lightning storm in Hell. They bolted from one woman's iconic sheen to the other; then, finally, fixing his, by now, hysterical gazeupon the Secretary. "You must know, by now, how sincere and submissive I can be given the merciful opportunity like when I say you have calmed me down, greatly neutralized me, sweetie-pie, er…I mean, madam…I mean, sir…I mean, boss, I mean, I no longer believe liberated women are nuts…I mean, I really do feel more receptive and imaginative than ever before...I mean I feel that you have re-constructed me... that is, I feel you've taken my tiger within and invited it to the circus cage...to wait for the gun and chair and the whip...without compromise...without complaint…"

"Shut your fritzie fool yap," said the Secretary. "Your bullshit blandishments arrive way too late," She pointed a fuchsia- colored fingernail at the man cowering at her feet. "Kiss my baby- calf boots," she snarled.

"No, no," he burbled, "I can't, I mean. . .oh, yes. . .I do so want to be enslaved by you! What I mean to say is...well, you can't…you cannot just..."

"Oh, but my dear Director, I can JUST! And, when you're properly dispatched, I will continue to JUST!" She was wagging her fingernail, again, like an elementary school disciplinarian. "You talk about imagination. You don't possess the imagination of a Crackerjack box Marquis de Sade, you disgusting, degenerate, impotent putz." She presently turned to acknowledge the encroaching circle of aluminum-clad women. "You ladies are aware that the time has come for his permanent evacuation!"

The Director only had time to scream twice.

• • •

Opposite page: **Artwork by T. Mike Walker**

KENNEDY
REAGAN BUSH '84
GOLDWATER
MILLER
POLITICAL
CONN
HOLY BIBLE
KENNEDY
FOR PRESIDENT
LBJ
SPEEDO

Artwork by Barye Phillips and L.R. Summers

DEATH GIRL

By James Gabriel

She remembered everything. It was her place to remember. She remembered herself and the way she was back then. Scared and held in the lonely denial of what was supposed to be life. She was trusting and she was naïve. Tony said he loved her, so she had been there for him. She was there for his cruelty and his infidelities, his lies and everything else that came with what she determined to be just a hard life.

She didn't push or force anything. In those days women didn't do that. In those days women did nothing, but spread their legs and cook and it was maddening. Tony said he wasn't ready to get married. Said he wasn't ready for kids or a family and though she was raised right and was a "good girl," she let him bring her to Chicago. He set her up in a small dive apartment and visited her regularly.

It wasn't entirely his fault. It was important she admitted at least that much to herself because Tony wasn't the first she trusted. Not by a long way. She was thin and pretty and had it a little rough growing up in her neighborhood. They were poor and when the first man came calling with money and a few gifts... Well, that's how the story goes. Then the next one, and the next, and before she knew it

CONTINUED, NEXT PAGE...

Art by Julie de Graag

...CONTINUED, FROM LAST PAGE

there were rumors about what kind of girl she was.

She crossed the bridge from Brooklyn to her job as a cocktail waitress and one day Tony walked in like he owned the whole joint. He had a smile like those types of guys do. "You're too pretty a dame to be in here selling things like that girlie." He said it so smooth. And she went so willingly.

She had never been a prostitute, but she had experience. She knew about men, what to do, and how to please. Honestly, most men weren't much more than circus morons in the bedroom anyway and Tony was no exception. When she started working on him, he lost control quickly, screamed out loud then started crying and mumbling something about his momma.

"I love you." He said, over and over again lying upon her breasts that night. He fell asleep like that and she believed him.

Tony wasn't very high up, but he was climbing fast. He wanted her to come back to Chicago with him. He said she would be taken care of and who didn't want to be taken care of. She was sold and came with nothing, but she didn't need anything because it was like he said. She was taken care of and it was wonderful.

All day in the apartment she read books, keeping them hidden away from Tony who, "don't like it when dames be gettin' too smart."

It had been a few months when he called one night, frantic. He needed her to get dressed in the black dress she

"... he lost control quickly, screamed out loud then started crying and mumbling..."

wore that time and the favor was simple. Do what she did to him, but she would be doing it to someone else.

She didn't want to, but he had to make amends for something or they might kill him. So, because he said he loved her and she did love him, she did it. The guy was fat and just as ignorant as Tony beneath the sheets, but he was clean and he didn't cry. He thanked her and left a hundred dollars when he left.

A gift he said it was.

Well, here she was naïve, because she thought it was nice

Artwork (opposite page) by Hannah Yaryan

"Tony was not the Tony she'd met. He was someone else.He was someone cruel."

of him to do that when she didn't ask.

Tony was happy and he said he loved her again. He bought her some nice things and they were back to normal for a month. Then it happened again. He said he needed her and she did it for him again. It was a different guy this time. He almost cried, but he sucked up his tears and hit her instead. Afterwards he left a hundred dollars as well. She was very confused about that, but a week later, it happened again with the first guy and the picture became a lot clearer.

After a while Tony didn't come around unless he needed her for that. Not for himself. Not anymore. She was soiled. She asked him questions he wouldn't answer and they didn't go out anymore. She understood what it all was. Tony made sure they were paying her and stopped paying for things. She got slapped and beaten, and read books when she was alone.

She was always alone.

Then one day it was over. Just over. They didn't call. Tony didn't call, but she knew where to find him and so she went.

Tony was not the Tony she'd met. He was someone else. He was someone cruel. "You don't ever come here you fucken broad, understand? Never!"

She was upset cried out, "You said that you loved me! And you cried like a baby the first time we were together!"

Tony looked at the other men seated around the table. They smirked at the comment and Tony's face changed. He grabbed her by the hair and dragged her into the alley where he beat her until she passed out. Then he put her in the dumpster.

It was dark when she came too. She dragged herself home limping, reaching a final decision.

In her apartment she turned off every light and lit every candle. Then sat in the kitchen with a straight razor, his straight razor. She sat thinking about everything that had happened. The razor was sharper than she thought it would be and when she cut her wrist it was deep, deeper than she thought it would be.

CONTINUED, NEXT PAGE...

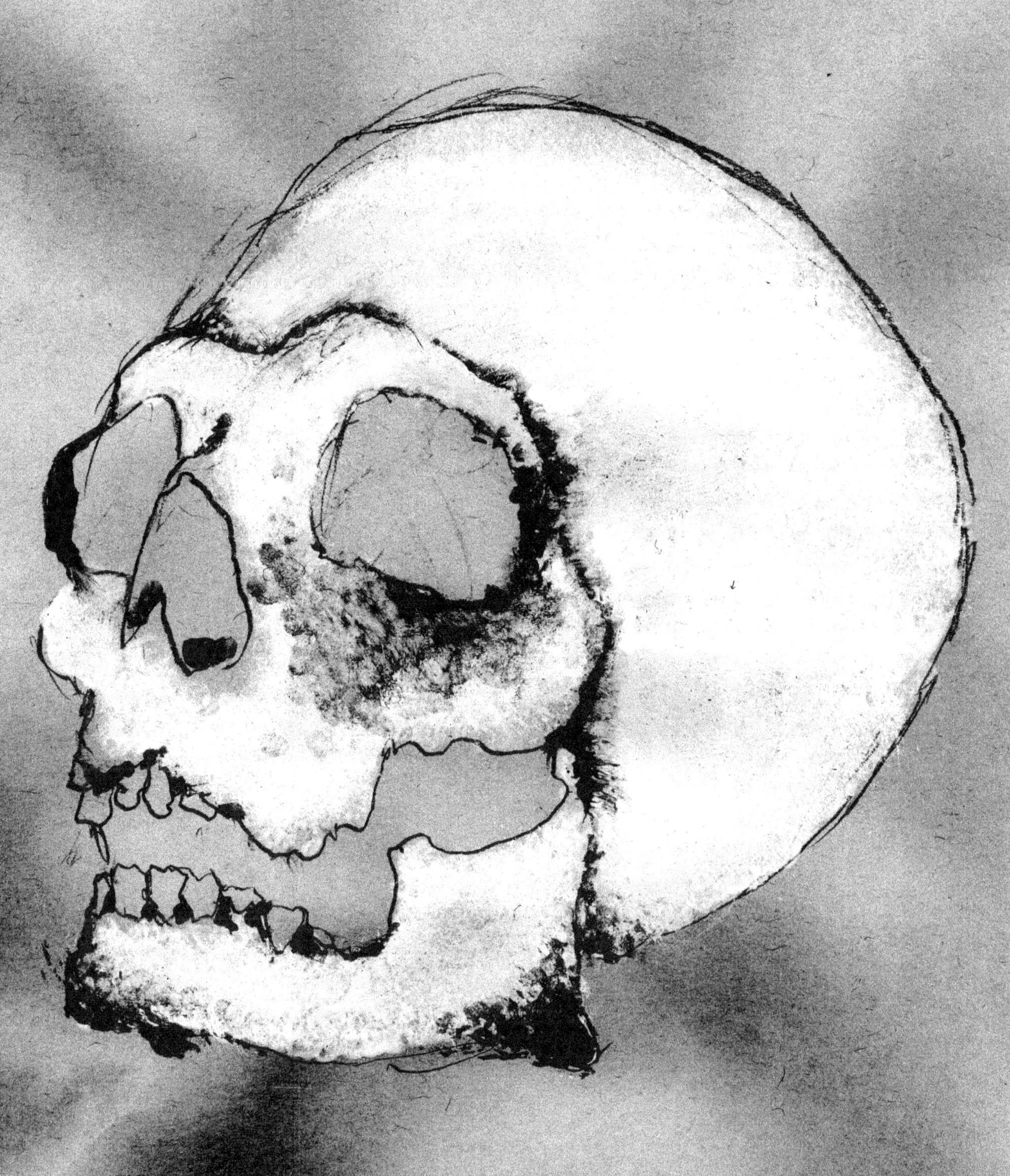

Artwork by Ernst Ludwig Kirchner

Artwork by Max Beckmann

...CONTINUED, FROM LAST PAGE

The blood spurted and the tendons popped as they were severed. Her hand went limp and she couldn't use it to cut her other wrist, but the one was enough, it had to be enough. In the candlelight she watched the blood flowing out of her wrist running like spilled sauce all over the kitchen table. She stared at her thumb continuing to twitch, her eyes blurring with tears.

The door to her apartment was locked and bolted. She made sure of that, but in her haze, she heard the lock click and the knob turn. The door swung open. A cold chilly wind entered the apartment and many of the candles blew and then disappeared. The curtains fluttered out and back again as the man stepped into her apartment.

The man looked like a circus ringmaster. Tall with an enormous belly. Skin deathly pale with dark, deep-set eyes that seemed to retreat into his skull. He was dressed in a black suit with tales over a blood red waistcoat held together by large gold buttons that shined brilliantly. A blood red bowler hat lined in black sat atop his head with a foot long jet-black crow's feather, sticking out of a black sash. He carried a red cane with a large golden skull handle. His two chubby middle fingers fondled the eye sockets as he held it.

She stood up from the table weak and terrified. Terror increasing her adrenaline caused the blood to flow faster. She held the razor up with her good hand, prepared for... For what? She didn't know.

"Do not be afraid my dear," the man spoke calmly. He passed with his bulk through the living room to the kitchen, pulled out the chair across from her and sat down, his

CONTINUED, NEXT PAGE...

"He used the golden death's head cane to push the clothes aside, revealing the great pile of books."

Artwork by Odilon Redon

...CONTINUED, FROM LAST PAGE

back straight.

She still held up the razor, but the loss of blood was starting to pull her down.

"Please," he motioned to the chair across from him. She stumbled forward as if pulled and sat down in the chair hard, slapping the razor down onto the table. Her head was getting fuzzy. She closed her eyes blinking a long heavy blink as ringmaster across from her said something she didn't understand.

The ringmaster cocked his head, "Well, this will never do." He announced fondling the eye sockets of his skull in frustration. He waved the back of his hand in her direction like a slap and power struck her, throwing her back in her seat. Her blood lay spilled all over the table like thick paint. The ringmaster reached over, grabbed her severed wrist and held it in the blood that began flowing back into her.

Her pulse quickened and the fog cleared from her head. Her sight sharpened and she saw the man sitting across from her almost for the first time. She knew who he was and why he was there.

He adjusted himself in his seat, clutching his cane and fingering the empty sockets of the golden skull. "Is that better?" he asked.

"Yes." She said nodding and beginning to cry. She cried her life, for Tony and his betrayal. She cried for her mother who told her sometimes it is hard work, but you do what you have to if you love him. Her mother had learned to excuse her father's cruelties and taught her daughter very well.

"Now there is simply no reason for that my dear." The man said pulling a blood red handkerchief from his coat pocket and passing it to her. She took it with her good hand and the man stood up. He began wandering around the apartment.

"I am certain it is this bad. So, I will not ask the simplistic questions," he said walking to the closet and opening door. He used the golden death's head cane to push the clothes aside, revealing the great pile of books. "Yes, I am certain it is as bad as it seems, but my dear you are unfulfilled and your unfulfillment is what has me stopping in for this most personal visit." He turned towards her seated at the table. "Is it that I am being clear?"

She nodded.

"Very well," he said releasing the clothes and closing the closet door with a strangely satisfying thud. He returned to the table and sat. Back straight, chubby fingers fondling the sockets of the skull. He sat scrutinizing her, "Is this the end you wish my dear?"

She began to cry again.

"No, no unnecessary," his voice deep with a soothing and calm that seemed reach inside and understand. She wiped her eyes with the red handkerchief.

"No fear." He said calmly. His eyes told the real story of his words through the darkness of his unblinking stare. "I can offer you something my dear. Something that is, extraordinary to this mundane existence I assure you. Power, yes to be certain power, but more than that." He paused

CONTINUED, NEXT PAGE...

...CONTINUED, FROM LAST PAGE

a moment, musing. "A fulfillment, the likes of which a woman in your position could not imagine in several lifetimes."

In his eyes she could see he meant what he said, and was speaking from experienced. She began to cry again.

"Yes! The alternative unfortunately is your current choice, but that too is not bad. You will most certainly find peace my dear. You will move on from this mortal coil and will find yourself on the other side, if that is your choice. I only make you this offer because of your want. Need. Something somewhere in the depths of you wants this. There is a seed of desire the likes of which you cannot fathom. That is all I can tell you, but of course, as with all things you have a choice." He fondled the eyes sockets and reached out with his free hand up to her awaiting her response.

She had been used for her kindness, which was probably the point. She was still pretty, but there was a sullen deadness in her gaze, which could be the reason why they stopped calling on her. She reached her good hand across the table to his.

"Bully my dear." He said smiling with a set of brilliant white teeth and reached for her hand.

His hand penetrated her. Reaching inside, it took hold of something else. She felt herself go, her body suddenly thudding to the table, dead and soulless. For a moment she was a wisp, out above them, seeing everything from outside herself and watching her dead body collapse to the kitchen floor. The walls became thin and she looked out to the city. It was night and the lights twinkled and the cars were out. She sensed rather than felt the chill, but more than that she was aware of all the emotions. There was a lot of fear, much more than joy or happiness which was there as well, though it was mostly reserved for mothers and youth. With the fear there was a great deal of pain and suffering and in this she felt purpose. It was faint and directionless, but purpose was there. There are people she could help and things she could do, if only....

A single light in the distance caught her attention. She turned and focused on what she knew to be Tony. She looked harder, her sight crossing the city to arrive beside him speaking to another girl. This girl was younger, much younger. Her smile opening doors and giving way to his charm and… suddenly she was back in the room hovering above herself.

"Oh, dear me, not like this," the man said. He stood quickly, his calm giving way to panic. He raised the cane, waving it in a wide circle encompassing the room in a dark mist. He looked around searching then focused on her above. "One moment my dear. I seem to have forgotten myself. Occupational hazard."

CONTINUED, NEXT PAGE...

...CONTINUED, FROM LAST PAGE

His hands made wild gestures reaching out to her and she felt herself being... gathered? Then he motioned towards her body and she shifted. A deep, beyond-earthly power suddenly surged through her and she stood, taking in an enormous inhalation of air. It was only a few feet but in that, feet she felt as if she traveled millions of miles,

"There was so much power at her disposal, the purpose she felt with it was almost overwhelming."

shafts of light and life passing around and through her until...

She was back in her body, fully conscious and aware of her surroundings and more than she was before. She looked down at her wrist watching it heal. She was both herself and the wisp. Aware of all that is and was beyond and more. There was so much power at her disposal, the purpose she felt with it was almost overwhelming.

The ringmaster sat staring across from her, searching to see if she was alright. She stood from the table, turning to examine her apartment mostly ignoring him. Absently she removed the clothes she was wearing and he ogled her nakedness casually. She crossed the room to the closet and took out the dress; the one Tony always asked her to wear. Jet black and held up by thin spaghetti straps. It draped over her body framing her nakedness in its perfection, fitting her better than it ever did before. She knew who she was now. She knew what she was and accepted the gift completely.

"Are you ready my dear?" The ringmaster asked. "There are things you must see and understand and albeit things you wish to complete."

She smiled and came forward barefoot almost gliding and took his hand. They moved to the window and were out. She looked back only once as they sailed into the night.

Tony didn't know what to make of her appearance the following day. She entered as if he hadn't beaten the shit out of her the day before, but she did look foxy in that black dress. It was the same one he'd bought, but he didn't remember it looking like that before. She was barefoot and

CONTINUED, NEXT PAGE...

Artwork by Max Beckmann

"Tables were overturned and guns were drawn and a lot of shots were fired. It was in all the papers. The headline read, 'Gangland.'"

...CONTINUED, FROM LAST PAGE

ready and the men seated around the table nudged each other, remembering what she'd said about him the other day.

Tony saw the look and stood. He moved on her fast. "You didn't get the fucking point yesterday is that it?" His intention now was to take her someplace and get one last one in, before finishing her off for good.

He grabbed her by nape of her neck and she allowed him to. She even cowered as he did it. She cowered the way she did before because she wanted to sample it. She wanted to feel. She wanted to remember who and what she was one last time. It didn't sicken her. She was still beautiful then, but she was not then who she was now.

Tony shoved her towards the door and suddenly she stopped, holding her place firm and statuesque.

"Come with me now, you fucking cunt!" Was the last thing Tony said before she raised her head to face him. It was the last thing before she truly became what she had become. Tony stared into the black endless obsidian depths of her eyes and began screaming. He cried like a baby again, for the last time.

Tables were overturned and guns were drawn and a lot of shots were fired. It was in all the papers. The headline read, "Gangland." There were pictures of the bodies, blood and brains decorating the walls. The police could never figure out how exactly they were killed. Perhaps it was a rival gang armed with baseball bats and swords, but that didn't make any sense. No one in the neighborhood heard or saw anything as per usual. The case was finally closed after the funerals, the great bouquets of flowers and the new bosses moved into the territory.

Illustration by Jery V. Stier

HERBERT WEST: REANIMATOR

By H.P. LOVECRAFT

Part I: From The Dark

Of Herbert West, who was my friend in college and in after life, I can speak only with extreme terror. This terror is not due altogether to the sinister manner of his recent disappearance, but was engendered by the whole nature of his life-work, and first gained its acute form more than seventeen years ago, when we were in the third year of our course at the Miskatonic University Medical School in Arkham. While he was with me, the wonder and diabolism of his experiments fascinated me utterly, and I was his closest companion. Now that he is gone and the spell is broken, the actual fear is greater. Memories and possibilities are ever more hideous than realities.

The first horrible incident of our acquaintance was the greatest shock I ever experienced, and it is only with reluctance that I repeat it. As I have said, it happened when we were in the medical school, where West had already made himself notorious through his wild theories on the nature of death and the possibility of overcoming it artificially. His views, which were widely ridiculed by the faculty and his fellow-students, hinged on the essentially mechanistic nature of life; and concerned means for operating the organic machinery of mankind by calculated chemical action after the failure of natural processes. In his experiments with various animating solutions he had killed and treated immense numbers of rabbits, guinea-pigs, cats, dogs, and monkeys, till he had become the prime nuisance of the college. Several times he had actually obtained signs of life in animals supposedly dead; in many cases violent signs; but he soon saw that the perfection of this process, if indeed possible, would necessarily involve a lifetime of research. It likewise became clear that, since the same solution never worked alike on different organic species, he would require human subjects for further and more specialised progress. It was here that he first came into conflict with the college authorities, and

"The first horrible incident of our acquaintance was the greatest shock I ever experienced, and it is only with reluctance that I repeat it."

CONTINUED, NEXT PAGE...

"I had always been exceptionally tolerant of West's pursuits, and we frequently discussed his theories, whose ramifications and corollaries were almost infinite."

Illustration by Fitz

...CONTINUED, FROM LAST PAGE

was debarred from future experiments by no less a dignitary than the dean of the medical school himself—the learned and benevolent Dr. Allan Halsey, whose work in behalf of the stricken is recalled by every old resident of Arkham.

I had always been exceptionally tolerant of West's pursuits, and we frequently discussed his theories, whose ramifications and corollaries were almost infinite. Holding with Haeckel that all life is a chemical and physical process, and that the so-called "soul" is a myth, my friend believed that artificial reanimation of the dead can depend only on the condition of the tissues; and that unless actual decomposition has set in, a corpse fully equipped with organs may with suitable measures be set going again in the peculiar fashion known as life. That the psychic or intellectual life might be impaired by the slight deterioration of sensitive brain-cells which even a short period of death would be apt to cause, West fully realised. It had at first been his hope to find a reagent which would restore vitality before the actual advent of death, and only repeated failures on animals had shewn him that the natural and artificial life-motions were incompatible. He then sought extreme freshness in his specimens, injecting his solutions into the blood immediately after the extinction of life. It was this circumstance which made the professors so carelessly sceptical, for they felt that true death had not occurred in any case. They did not stop to view the matter closely and reasoningly.

It was not long after the faculty had interdicted his work that West confided to me his resolution to get fresh human bodies in some manner, and continue in secret the experiments he could no longer perform openly. To hear him discussing ways and means was rather ghastly, for at the college we had never procured anatomical specimens ourselves. Whenever the morgue proved inadequate, two local laborers attended to this matter, and they were seldom questioned. West was

CONTINUED, NEXT PAGE...

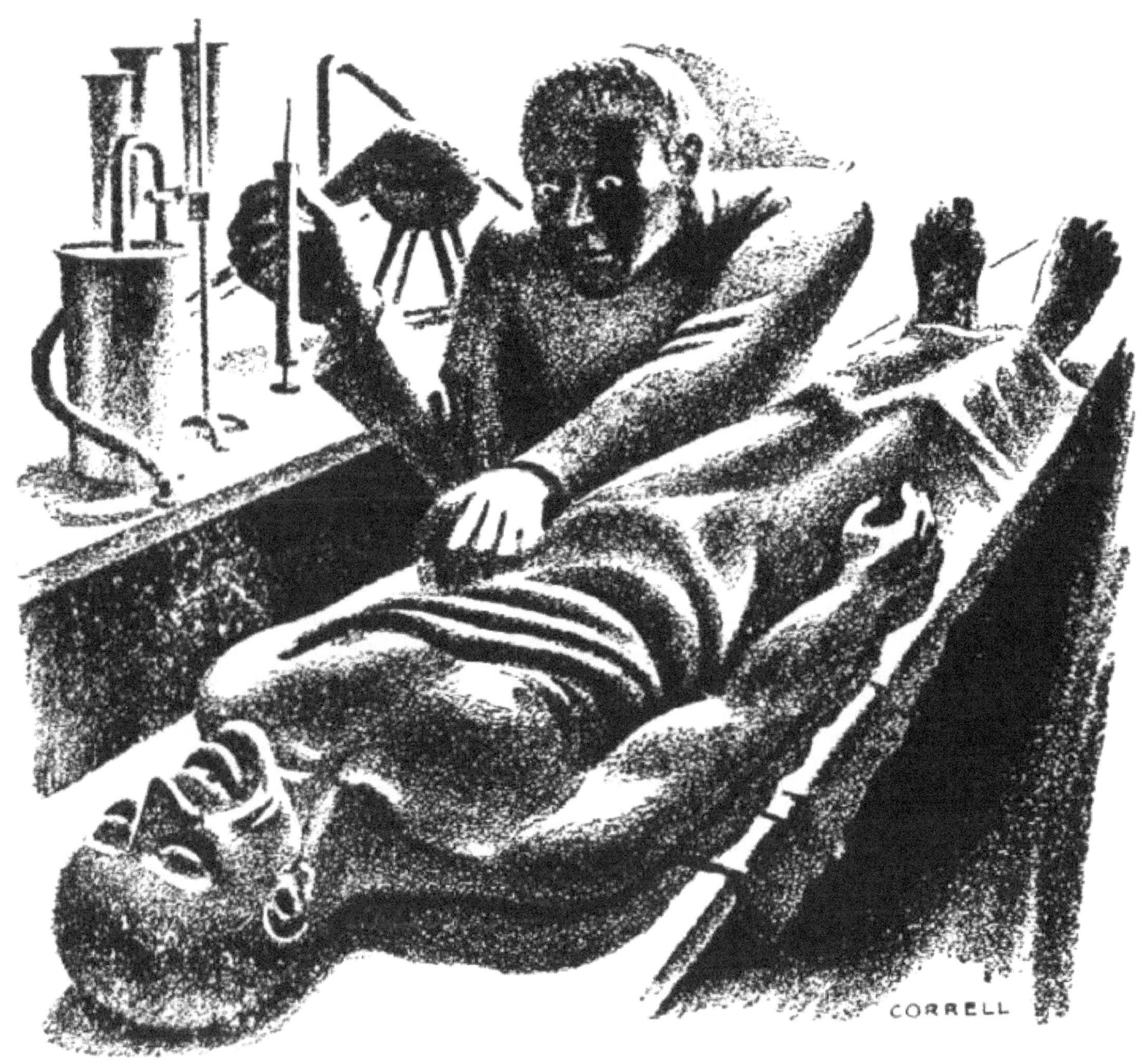

Illustration by Richard V. Correll

"It was not long after the faculty had interdicted his work that West confided to me his resolution to get fresh human bodies in some manner, and continue in secret the experiments he could no longer perform openly."

"The process of unearthing was slow and sordid—it might have been gruesomely poetical if we had been artists instead of scientists"

...CONTINUED, FROM LAST PAGE

then a small, slender, spectacled youth with delicate features, yellow hair, pale blue eyes, and a soft voice, and it was uncanny to hear him dwelling on the relative merits of Christchurch Cemetery and the potter's field. We finally decided on the potter's field, because practically every body in Christchurch was embalmed; a thing of course ruinous to West's researches.

I was by this time his active and enthralled assistant, and helped him make all his decisions, not only concerning the source of bodies but concerning a suitable place for our loathsome work. It was I who thought of the deserted Chapman farmhouse beyond Meadow Hill, where we fitted up on the ground floor an operating room and a laboratory, each with dark curtains to conceal our midnight doings. The place was far from any road, and in sight of no other house, yet precautions were none the less necessary; since rumours of strange lights, started by chance nocturnal roamers, would soon bring disaster on our enterprise. It was agreed to call the whole thing a chemical laboratory if discovery should occur. Gradually we equipped our sinister haunt of science with materials either purchased in Boston or quietly borrowed from the college—materials carefully made unrecognisable save to expert eyes—and provided spades and picks for the many burials we should have to make in the cellar. At the college we used an incinerator, but the apparatus was too costly for our unauthorised laboratory. Bodies were always a nuisance—even the small guinea-pig bodies from the slight clandestine experiments in West's room at the boarding-house.

We followed the local death-notices like ghouls, for our specimens demanded particular qualities. What we wanted were corpses interred soon after death and without artificial preservation; preferably free from malforming disease, and certainly with all organs present. Accident victims were our best hope. Not for many weeks did we hear of anything suitable; though we talked with morgue and hospital authorities, ostensibly in the college's interest, as often as we could without exciting suspicion. We found that the college had first choice in every case, so that it might be necessary to remain in Arkham during the summer, when only the limited summer-school classes were held. In the end, though, luck favoured us; for one day we heard of an almost ideal case in the potter's field; a brawny young workman drowned only the morning before in Sumner's Pond, and buried at the town's expense without delay or embalming. That afternoon we found the new grave, and determined to begin work soon after midnight.

It was a repulsive task that we undertook in the black small hours, even though we lacked at that time the special horror of graveyards which later experiences brought to us. We carried spades and oil dark lanterns, for although electric torches were then manufactured, they were not as satisfactory as the tungsten contrivances of today. The process of unearthing was slow and sordid—it might have been gruesomely poetical if we had been artists instead of scientists—and we were glad when our spades struck wood. When the pine box was fully uncovered West scrambled down and removed the lid, dragging out and propping up the contents. I reached down and hauled the contents out of the grave, and then both toiled hard to restore the spot to its former appearance. The affair made us rather nervous, especially the stiff form and vacant face of our first trophy, but we managed to remove all traces of our visit. When we had patted down the last shovelful of earth we put the specimen in a canvas sack and set out for the old Chapman place beyond Meadow Hill.

On an improvised dissecting-table in the old farmhouse, by the light of a powerful acetylene lamp, the specimen was not very spectral looking. It had been a sturdy and apparently unimaginative youth of wholesome plebeian type—large-framed, grey-eyed, and brown-haired—a sound animal without psychological subtleties, and probably having vital processes of the simplest and healthiest sort. Now, with the eyes closed, it looked more asleep than dead; though the expert test of my friend soon left no doubt on that score. We had at

CONTINUED, NEXT PAGE...

Illustration by Fitz

...CONTINUED, FROM LAST PAGE

last what West had always longed for—a real dead man of the ideal kind, ready for the solution as prepared according to the most careful calculations and theories for human use. The tension on our part became very great. We knew that there was scarcely a chance for anything like complete success, and could not avoid hideous fears at possible grotesque results of partial animation. Especially were we apprehensive concerning the mind and impulses of the creature, since in the space following death some of the more delicate cerebral cells might well have suffered deterioration. I, myself, still held some curious notions about the traditional "soul" of man, and felt an awe at the secrets that might be told by one returning from the dead. I wondered what sights this placid youth might have seen in inaccessible spheres, and what he could relate if fully restored to life. But my wonder was not overwhelming, since for the most part I shared the materialism of my friend. He was calmer than I as he forced a large quantity of his fluid into a vein of the body's arm, immediately binding the incision securely.

The waiting was gruesome, but West never faltered. Every now and then he applied his stethoscope to the specimen, and bore the negative results philosophically. After about three-quarters of an hour without the least sign of life he disappointedly pronounced the solution inadequate, but determined to make the most of his opportunity and try one change in the formula before disposing of his ghastly prize. We had that afternoon dug a grave in the cellar, and would have to fill it by dawn—for although we had fixed a lock on the house we wished to shun even the remotest risk of a ghoulish discovery. Besides, the body would not be even approximately fresh the next night. So taking the solitary acetylene lamp into the adjacent laboratory, we left our silent guest on the slab in the dark, and bent every energy to the mixing of a new solution; the weighing and measuring supervised by West with an almost fanatical care.

The awful event was very sudden, and wholly unexpected. I was pouring something from one test-tube to another, and West was busy over the alcohol blast-lamp which had to answer for a Bunsen burner in this gasless edifice, when from the pitch-black room we had left there burst the most appalling and daemoniac succession of cries that either of us had ever heard. Not more unutterable could have been the chaos of hellish sound if the pit itself had opened to release the agony of the damned, for in one inconceivable cacophony was centred all the supernal terror and unnatural despair of animate nature. Human it could not have been—it is not in man to make such sounds—and without a thought of our late employment or its possible discovery both West and I leaped to the nearest window like stricken animals; overturning tubes, lamp, and retorts, and vaulting madly into the starred abyss of the rural night. I think we screamed ourselves as we stumbled frantically toward the town, though as we reached the outskirts we put on a semblance of restraint—just enough to seem like belated revellers staggering home from a debauch.

"We knew that there was scarcely a chance for anything like complete success, and could not avoid hideous fears at possible grotesque results of partial animation. Especially were we apprehensive concerning the mind and impulses of the creature..."

We did not separate, but managed to get to West's room, where we whispered with the gas up until dawn. By then we had calmed ourselves a little with rational theories and plans for investigation, so that we could sleep through the day—classes being disregarded. But that evening two items in the paper, wholly unrelated, made it again impossible for us to sleep. The old deserted Chapman house had inexplicably burned to an amorphous heap of ashes; that we could understand because of the upset lamp. Also, an attempt had been made to disturb a new grave in the potter's field, as if by futile and spadeless clawing at the earth. That we could not understand, for we had patted down the mould very carefully.

And for seventeen years after that West would look frequently over his shoulder, and complain of fancied footsteps behind him. Now he has disappeared.

***

Illustration by Fitz

POETRY PLANET

WHERE WORDSMITHS RULE THE WORLD

Illustration by Hannes Bok

ELLYN MAYBE
SCIENCE POEM

Illustration by Shari Weisberg

I started thinking about the wonder of words.

I've always been a good speller
        but I thought a second about how science sounded.

I knew it was s-c-i-e-n-c-e
        but it sounded sign—ence
        or even psy—ence.

And I thought wow maybe if people
        looked at the psychological impact
        of inventing cause isn't science
        sort of making known what's here
        in some other form and combining,
        inventing the new fresh
        or the old fresh?

And a sign, a thoughtful responsible
        pondering sigh, might create a whole new outlook for science.

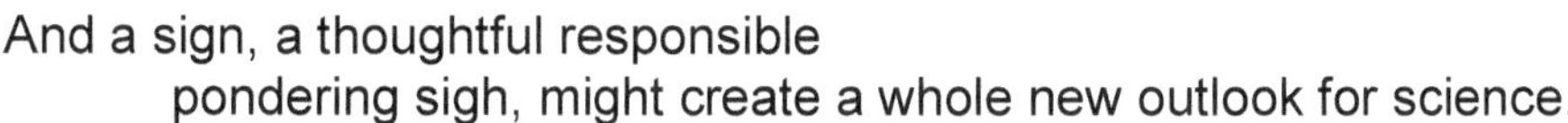

I think science is the microcosm of the human spirit.

People probably felt the psychological bomb
        inside their heads, inside their hearts
        caused by maybe bad uncaring parents
        or not being invited to dance
        or what not, before they could
        invent the bomb that kills
        inward and outward and leaves
        buildings unharmed.

I've heard about the guilt of scientists,
        I haven't heard too much about the guilt of politicians.

Inventions are sort of weird,
        many take us far away from being human
        Like bosses. I mean it sort of takes the
        "all men are created equal" thing
        and where is the woman in that
        and says o.k. you're created equal
        but at the moment of conception
        it's the bosses and the who will be bossed
        the haves and the have nots, etc.

Science is the invention of a weight scale
        a machine with numbers that
        turns people crazy, tears at self-esteem

CONTINUED, NEXT PAGE...

...CONTINUED, FROM LAST PAGE

but is it the numbers
or the people that serve
as mean weight guessers
at the carnival of planet earth.

Now science is not all bad,
not by a long shot,
if it weren't for phonograph
I wouldn't be able to hear
Idiot Wind by Bob Dylan unless
I went to a concert
and he felt like doing it
and who knows.

If it weren't' for science
I couldn't stay up day and night listening to KPFK.

So science has many good things going
it's how it's used.

Science is as vulnerable as any other human thing.

It's supply and demand.

If the people look like they're going
to be having a war, war toys
and war bumperstickers and
other stuff will be invented.

On the other hand, people will rise
with poetry and songs and wisdom
to tilt back the world.

Unfortunately, ego gets in the way.
Science says, wow!
that is such a fantastic television set
but I can make a bigger better T.V. set
than the scientist with the master's degree
plus my T.V. set will have a swimming pool inside
and be fluent in 39 languages.

And this T.V. will make me famous
I'll be on T.V.

And one person
the richest person in the world
buys the T.V. and he is the only one
who can afford this "miracle."

And he decides to invite one person over to watch some documentaries.

CONTINUED, NEXT PAGE...

...CONTINUED, FROM LAST PAGE

An this one person is starving
because she thinks the richest man
will like her cause she's thin.

So when a commercial comes on for soup
she rubs her hand against the screen
thinking this magic machine will feed her.

The man slaps her for getting fingerprints
on the screen and so she get up
too desperate to leave cause
if he's so rich, he must be the best man.

So she realizes this T.V. has a bunk bed
so she lays inside the T.V.
trying to sleep but the man says
your breasts are making
a shadow on the screen
and she vows to eat less
than nothing tomorrow.

So she says
this machine doesn't give food
doesn't give shelter
what does it give?

He said
it gives me an excuse to pretend you're not there.

And she walked slowly to the pool part
of the T.V. set and kept walking.

And he flipped channels
thinking he could escape life by UHF.

But the woman was swimming on T.V. now.

She was famous.
He was rich.
Drowning in different water.

They didn't have anything they needed.
lots of people told them they had it all.

I hear these T.V. sets have become affordable now.

---ellyn maybe

Art by Karl Wiener ***(Opposite page)***

PJ SWIFT
777

You feeling lucky? Those were words I liked to repeat to myself as I played the onscreen slot machine game on the back of the seat in front of me as I was flying to Calcutta. I heard that line in a movie somewhere, and it stuck with me each time I played a silly game of chance, which wasn't often. I was hoping to strike the triple 777, and since this game was designed primarily to grant distraction and pleasure I hit 777 several times. But knowing that the game was rigged to please me, didn't make me feel all that lucky.

Sealed in the backseat of a luxury sedan, and later delivered to a pristine and luxuriant hotel, I did feel lucky. The few glimpses I caught of life outside on the colorful, crowded streets of Calcutta, caused me to reflect where fate had delivered me, and where it had led others.

I was in the city for business, but I am not completely unadventurous or without sentiment. A friend from my previous destination whom I had met for dinner asked me to deliver a book to his old mentor, a respected scholar of Bengali poetry in Calcutta. Despite my busy schedule, I agreed to devote a couple of hours to this task. If nothing else this was a chance to meet a real person in this enchanted city. Gliding through the streets in my gilded transport, as masses of lives foreign to mine swarmed in their daily business, I again considered thoughts along the lines of do I feel lucky. What power had granted me this life, and not one of those out there that I imagined more burdened, less joyful and less blessed than mine. We arrived at my destination and I was surprised to realize the street number, 777. I did feel lucky.

The scholar, an older, stately man, wearing a heavy colorful sweater, large glasses, and holding a cane, received me graciously and sat me down for tea. His apartment was modest, filled with the warmth of his scholarship and books. His chair was rather meager and frail, but he sat as if on a throne, granting a benign and enlightened audience. Though his face was placid and still, his eyes, direct and unwavering, cast a radiant smile. There was no small-talk as he immediately pulled me into an involved intellectual discussion on reincarnation, one in which, surprisingly, I soon became an active contributor. As I responded to his queries on the topic, I enthusiastically provided suppositions of my own. I opined that perhaps each one of us only has an awareness of a limited total number of people. What if that really were only the number of souls in existence, and not only that, but that each one of us has each been one of those people, thereby living in this world countless times in countless permutations. Destiny spins like a slot machine and sometimes, every now or then, we strike 777. The scholar retained the same still regal pose. Unmoving, his eyes radiating. He had allowed me to do all the talking. Finally, he nodded. It was very interesting what I had just noted. He took the book that I had brought him, a rather heavy hardcover, and excused himself for a moment. He wanted to place this in another room, and if I wouldn't mind, briefly attend to other business. I sat still in my chair, comfortable, feeling at rest. And I waited, and waited, and still he did not return. I waited, growing more comfortable, sedate, contemplative.

The doorbell rang. A foreigner, a younger man, had arrived with a gift. I adjusted my large glasses, straightened my heavy colorful sweater, and walked with my cane to greet him.

ART BY WASSILY KANDINSKY

Illustration by Karl Wiener

Scratch

by Andrew Orillion

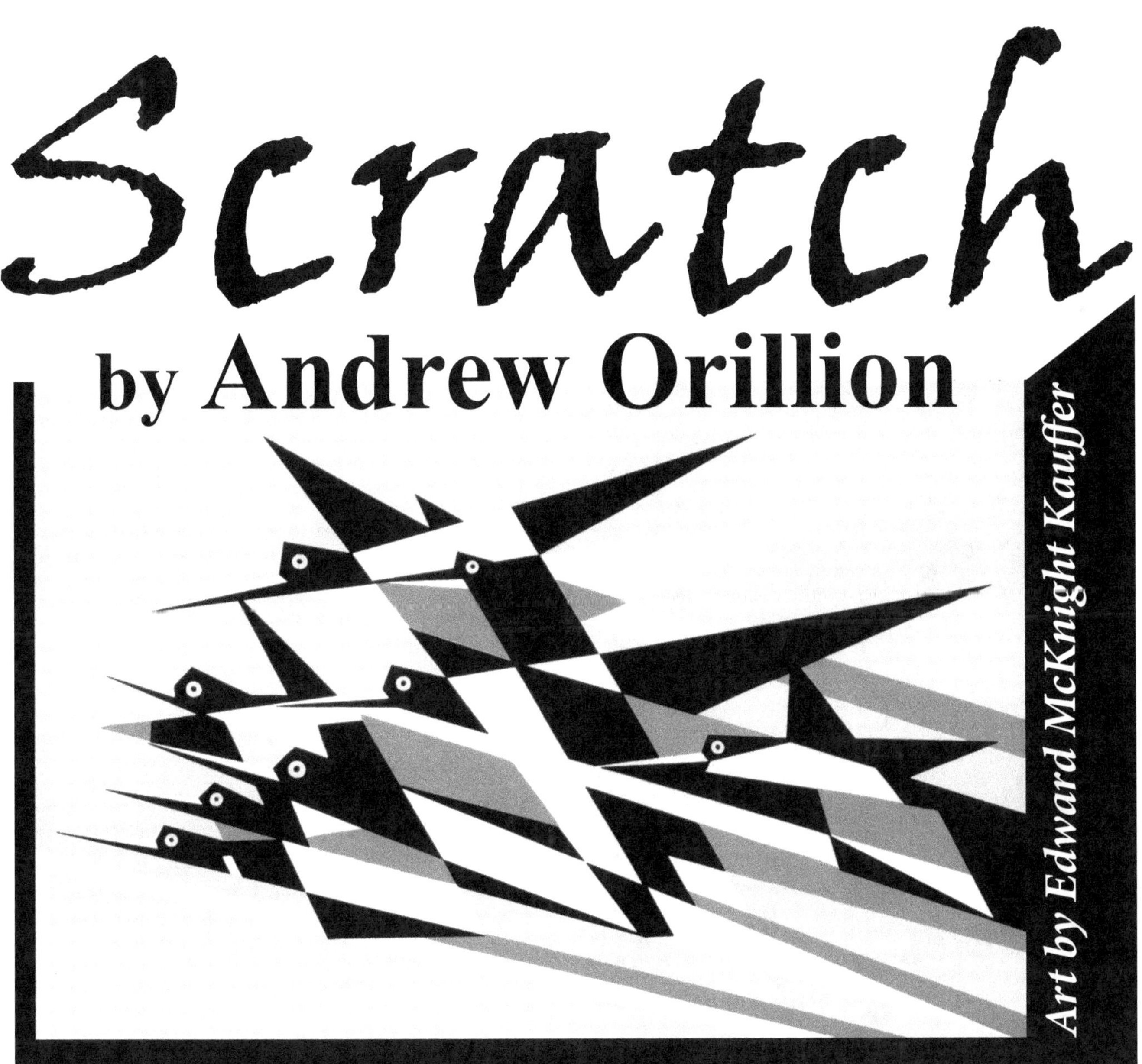

Art by Edward McKnight Kauffer

"Alvin lightly banged his fist on the wall a few times. Maybe whatever was inside could be scared off."

Alvin was playing a game on his PC the first time he heard it.

SCRATCH. SCRATCH.

He usually played with headphones on, but this was a real-time strategy game, not an FPS or a survival horror game that required full immersion. His roommate/landlord, Eric, had just started a 14-day quarantine at his girlfriend's house, so headphones weren't necessary. They sat unused on the desk charging station.

Alvin paused the game and listened for the sound again. He waited. Nothing. Just the fan's hum in the PC's tricked out case. Alvin shrugged and went back to his game.

Gaming was one of the few pleasures Alvin had in his life at the moment. Worked a low wage job, rented a one-room "apartment" in a house, and hadn't had a girlfriend in years. Now, thanks to the pandemic, his job was gone, and dating was a lost cause. His room and PC were all he had. It was a quiet, peaceful life

CONTINUED, NEXT PAGE...

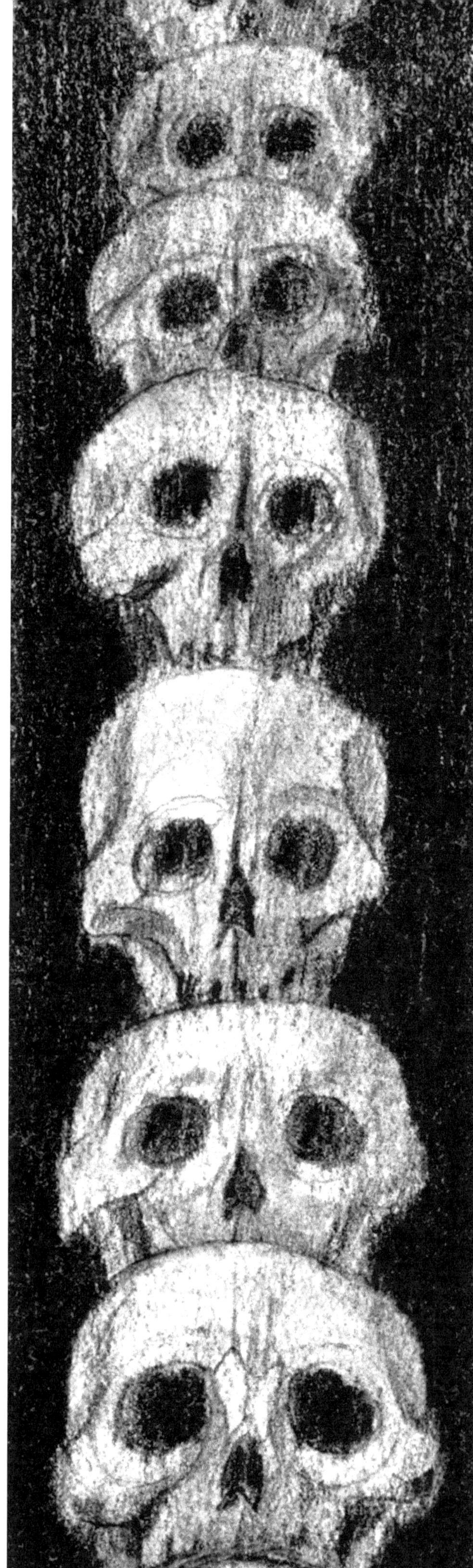

SCRATCH CONTINUED, FROM LAST PAGE

made even more so by the pandemic. Alvin had barely left the house in a month, getting everything he needed delivered. Peace and quiet.

SCRATCH. SCRATCH.

Alvin paused the game again and looked around the room.

"What the hell is that?" Alvin said.

He pushed his chair back and searched the room for the source of the noise. There was nothing obvious. Nothing had fallen down –no loose papers flapping in a draft. Air conditioning running, but that wasn't the source. Alvin checked the window blinds at the other end of the room. Sometimes they rattled against the frame or the window itself. Nothing. Blinds were stiff and unwavering. Alvin pulled the cord and brought the blinds up to the top, just to be sure.

He went back to his game.

His rolling chair squeaked as he leaned back.

Mystery solved, Alvin thought.

Squeaked the chair a few more times for good measure. Vowed to check the garage for some 3-in-1 Oil tomorrow morning. Even if he lived alone, there was no need to have a squeaky chair.

Alvin stayed at his computer until his eyes grew heavy, and he started losing feeling in his fingers. He didn't check to see what time it was. It was late, very late. His body was going into shut down mode. Alvin turned off his computer, tossed his clothes on the floor, and crawled into bed. He took a deep breath and was out.

SCRATCH. SCRATCH.

Alvin opened his eyes. The room was dark, even with the window blinds rolled up. The windows in his room faced east, so the sun usually woke him up. He couldn't have been asleep for long because it was still dark. Alvin grabbed his phone and checked the time. Almost three a.m… He listened for the sound again. His own shallow breathing and the rustle of bed-sheets were all he heard. Air conditioning wasn't even running.

SCRATCH. SCRATCH.

Alvin grabbed his phone and activated the light. He lit up his room, but there was nothing out of the ordinary, just like before.

SCRATCH. SCRATCH.

It was coming from inside the room, but not inside the room. A strange duality that took Alvin's exhausted brain a few moments to come to terms with. "It's coming from outside. Goddamn it, I'm going to have to get up for this," Alvin said out loud to himself as he slipped on his boxer shorts and left his room. It

SCRATCH CONTINUED, NEXT PAGE...

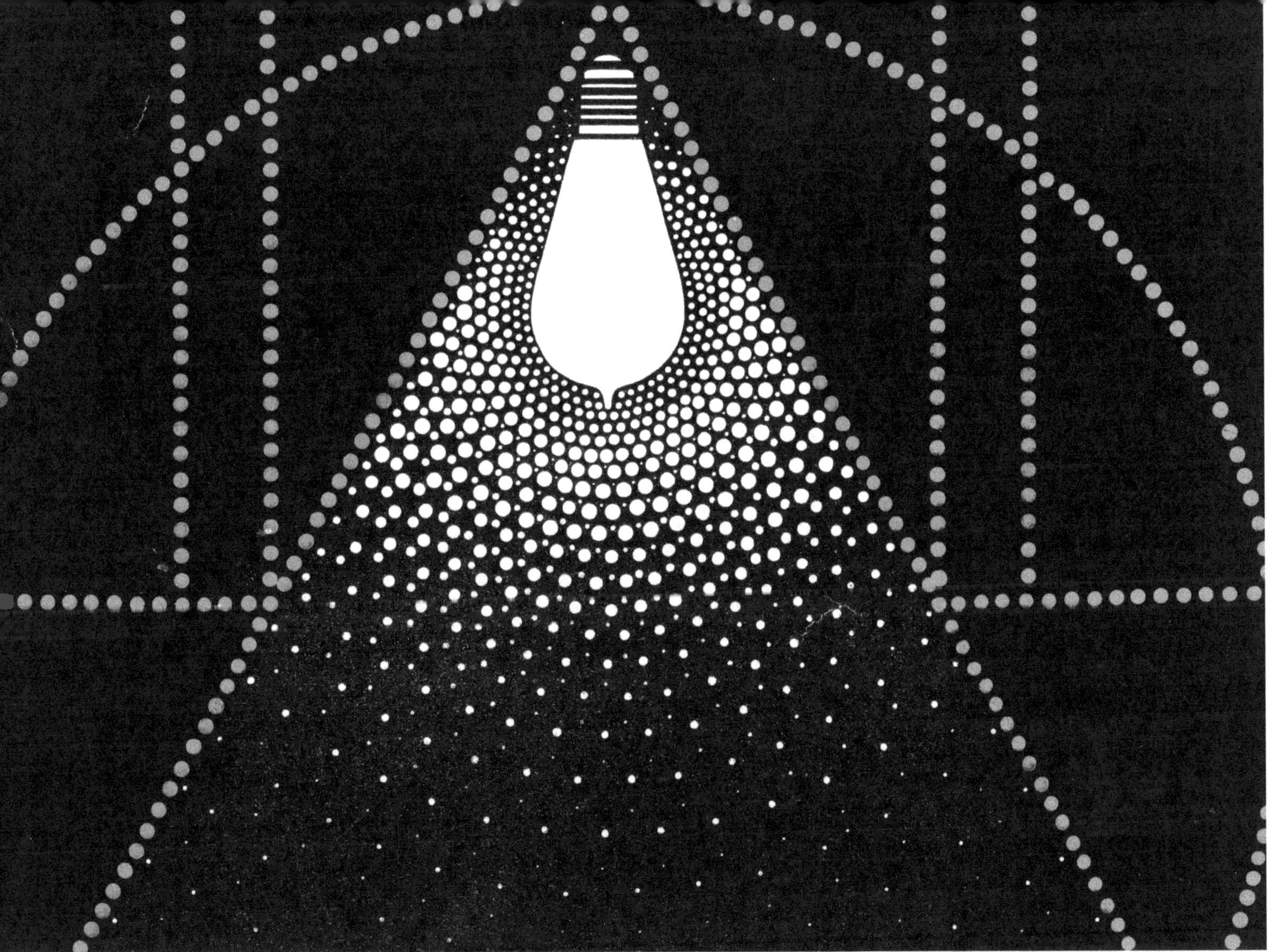

Art by Peter Behrens

SCRATCH CONTINUED, FROM LAST PAGE

was summer, so he wouldn't need much more.

SCRATCH. SCRATCH.

Definitely coming from outside. Alvin left his room at the back of the house and headed for the garage. He wanted to grab a flashlight and double-check that Eric hadn't come back. The garage was empty. Alvin was still alone in the house. Alone in the world, pretty much. He took a flashlight, slipped on a pair of sandals he kept by the front door for quick trips to the mailbox, and such and went outside to check around the house.

Nothing. No animals scurrying away. No footprints or other signs of disturbance. Not that Alvin expected to find such things, his neighborhood was very safe. Still, he would've liked to have seen something, anything to let him know what he'd heard.

SCRATCH. SCRATCH.

Alvin whipped around and scanned the flashlight over the wall. Nothing. He turned around, passed the beam over the small backyard. The flashlight illuminated the grass, the lone tree, and some empty planters that marked Eric's one and only attempt to develop a green thumb. The yard was empty. Alvin was the only living thing in the yard.

SCRATCH. SCRATCH.

He turned back to the wall outside his room. He ran the flashlight up and down the wall. It was undamaged, and nothing was crawling across it. He put his ear to the wall.

SCRATCH. SCRATCH.

It was inside. Not inside the room, inside the wall.

SCRATCH. SCRATCH.

Definitely, inside the wall of his room. The wall he had his desk against. Alvin checked the ground for any signs of disturbed earth or holes at the wall's base where a rat or squirrel might get in. The dirt was undisturbed, and the wall was intact.

SCRATCH CONTINUED, NEXT PAGE...

Art by Karl Wiener

SCRATCH CONTINUED, FROM LAST PAGE

SCRATCH. SCRATCH.

"It must have gotten in some other way. Maybe through the roof."

Alvin lightly banged his fist on the wall a few times. Maybe whatever was inside could be scared off. He waited outside by the wall listening for the scratching sound. Nothing. He waited a little longer, more nothing. Satisfied, Alvin went back inside. He kept the flashlight, just in case. He crawled under the covers, took deep breathes to slow his heart rate, felt his body get heavy. Just before he drifted off, he thought he heard scratching again.

The next morning, Alvin was back at his PC, playing the same game as before. It's not like he had anything else to do. Everything was closed because of the pandemic, and Alvin wasn't the outdoorsy type anyway. His room was his world, but he didn't stay there all day. There was a nice living room with a sizable TV that Alvin liked to hook his laptop into. Plus, there was the kitchen with all the modern amenities. Alvin was returning from the kitchen with a mid-morning snack of cheese and saltines when he heard it.

SCRATCH. SCRATCH.

As before, it was in the wall. He set his plate down, got on his hands, and knees and checked the wall.

SCRATCH. SCRATCH.

It was coming from the base of the wall, ground level. The noise continued.

SCRATCH. SCRATCH.

Alvin banged on the wall, same as last night, and got the same result. The noise stopped. He sat down, started munching, and web surfing. A nice break from the game. He was down to his last few saltines and cheese slices when it came back.

SCRATCH. SCRATCH.

Alvin didn't get up. He kicked the wall and went back to eating.

SCRATCH. SCRATCH.

Alvin was getting annoyed. He left his room, put on his sandals, and headed to the backyard to check the wall. It was a beautiful day, cloudless and so blue it almost hurt to look at it. It would've been the perfect day for a beach trip, a hike through the woods, or just a stroll around the neighborhood. Alvin briefly felt

SCRATCH CONTINUED, NEXT PAGE...

Art by Rudolf Bauer

SCRATCH CONTINUED, FROM LAST PAGE

guilty about spending his day inside, in front a screen that both connected and separated him from the world. Then he remembered the quarantine; everything was closed anyway, so there was no point in feeling guilty. Inside was where it's at.

As long nothing outside was trying to get inside.

But, something was, and Alvin saw the evidence. Earth had been disturbed at the base of the wall. Something had been digging under the foundation. Alvin wondered why it wasn't there last night when he first heard the scratching sound. He'd looked for holes in the walls or loose dirt but hadn't seen anything.

Probably just missed it in the dark. Maybe it filled in the hole after it left? Maybe whatever it is, it was getting in some other way before, and now it's switched to this?

Ultimately, it didn't matter how it got in; it just had to leave. Alvin went to the garage and got a shovel to fill in the tiny hole. While he was there, he looked to see if his landlord had any rat poison lying around. Eric was a handyman and had a garage full of every type of tool and trinket imaginable. Wrenches, screwdrivers, clippers, trimmers, hammers, pumps, and paddles. There were drawers filled with nuts, bolts, and screws of every shape and size imaginable. If there was a tool for the job, Eric had it somewhere.

Alvin found the rat poison on a shelf next to a can of foam insulation and a paint thinner tub. Poison was a last resort. He didn't care if the offending animal died; he just didn't want it to die in the walls. That would create a whole other set of problems. He put the poison back and returned to the wall. He listened for the sound, but all he heard was the AC. He filled in the hole and piled more loose dirt around the area. He thought about returning the shovel to the garage, Eric was a stickler for such things, but he decided to leave it in the backyard in case he needed to use it again.

It started again that night.

SCRATCH. SCRATCH. SCRATCH.

Alvin put on his headphones and tried to ignore the sound. He could still hear it.

SCRATCH. SCRATCH. SCRATCH.

He turned up the sound. He could still hear it. Faint but there. He turned up the sound a little more and tried to focus on the game.

Take your mind off of it. Whatever's in there can't scratch at the wall all night. It'll stop eventually.

SCRATCH. SCRATCH. SCRATCH.

Why didn't I invest in noise-cancelling headphones?

SCRATCH. SCRATCH. SCRATCH. SCRATCH. SCRATCH. SCRATCH.

Artwork by Wayne White

Alvin kept playing as the scratching continued. It was after midnight before it finally stopped. He took off his headphones and listened to the beautiful silence that hung over his room. The sound was gone, and it was time for bed. He could've stayed up longer, it's not like he had to get up early for work, but his bed called to him in soft, gentle tones. He left his clothes on the floor and crawled into bed.

SCRATCH. SCRATCH. SCRATCH.

It was back. Alvin checked the time and realized he'd only been asleep two hours. He rolled away from the window and tried to ignore the sound.

SCRATCH. SCRATCH. SCRATCH.

He kept trying to ignore it. Maybe he could fall asleep in between the scratches. The sound died down. Alvin closed his eyes, took a deep breath, and soon felt his body get light.

SCRATCH. SCRATCH. SCRATCH.

He tried again –deep breath. Relax. Almost there.

SCRATCH. SCRATCH. SCRATCH.

SCRATCH CONTINUED, NEXT PAGE...

Artwork by Karl Wiener

Artwork by Wayne White

SCRATCH CONTINUED, FROM LAST PAGE

It's nothing bad. Just an animal in the wall. It can't hurt you or get to you. It's just noise. Block it out.

SCRATCH. SCRATCH. SCRATCH.

It was just noise in the same way a jackhammer or fingernails on a chalkboard were just noises. He couldn't just ignore it. As much as he wanted to. There was simply no way to shut the sound out or live with it. He got out of bed and gently kicked the wall where the sound was coming from.

SCRATCH. SCRATCH. SCRATCH.

He kicked the wall again, and it stopped. He went back to bed and tried to sleep, but he was too wound up. He stared at the ceiling, tossed and turned for a long time before almost falling asleep.

SCRATCH. SCRATCH. SCRATCH.

Alvin couldn't take it anymore. He threw off the sheets and went outside.

The hole under the wall was back.

It was back.

Alvin could hear the scratching. It was in the walls –no doubt about it. Alvin picked up the shovel and banged it against the wall. Not too hard. He didn't want to damage anything. He just wanted to scare away whatever was in the wall. The scratching stopped. Alvin waited.

SCRATCH. SCRATCH. SCRATCH.

He smacked the shovel against the wall again. He waited in the cold night air. No scratching. Nothing. He left the shovel in the backyard and returned to bed –no more scratching.

Quiet the next night. Alvin returned the shovel, filled back in the dirt, and plugged every little crack he could find with the can of spray foam. The scratching may have ended, but he didn't want a repeat. Alvin returned to his regular routine and slept like a baby. The sound had been a short-lived annoyance, but little else. His sleep schedule had been thrown off, but that didn't really matter. It's not like he had to be up—

SCRATCH. SCRATCH. SCRATCH.

He hadn't scared off whatever it was. It was back. Now earlier in the evening. Alvin feared he'd have to listen to the sound all night. He kicked the wall.

SCRATCH. SCRATCH. SCRATCH.

Alvin went to the garage, grabbed the shovel and the flashlight. He checked the foundation. Nothing. No new holes. Foam isolation was undisturbed –no scratching sound.

Maybe I'm hearing things? Maybe I've been cooped up too long?

SCRATCH. SCRATCH. SCRATCH.

Clear as day. He banged the shovel against the wall where he heard the noise. A little harder than before.

SCRATCH. SCRATCH. SCRATCH.

He banged the shovel into the wall again. Probably loud enough to wake the neighbors.

"Get out! Get out of my wall!" Alvin hissed. He smacked the wall a few more times for effect.

SCRATCH. SCRATCH. SCRATCH.

The shovel met the wall again. And again. And again. Alvin wanted to hit the wall again, but he was worried about breaking it. He wasn't to that point yet but a few more nights of this, and he might be. The scratching stopped. Alvin tapped the wall a few more times. He propped the shovel against the wall. Then, retreated inside.

His adrenaline was pumping. He'd have to calm down before sleep would come. He parked in the living room and switched the TV on. Not much on at 2:30 am –just a lot of reruns, infomercials, more infomercials. As Alvin flipped through the channels, the sound on the TV went off in between stations. During

SCRATCH CONTINUED, NEXT PAGE...

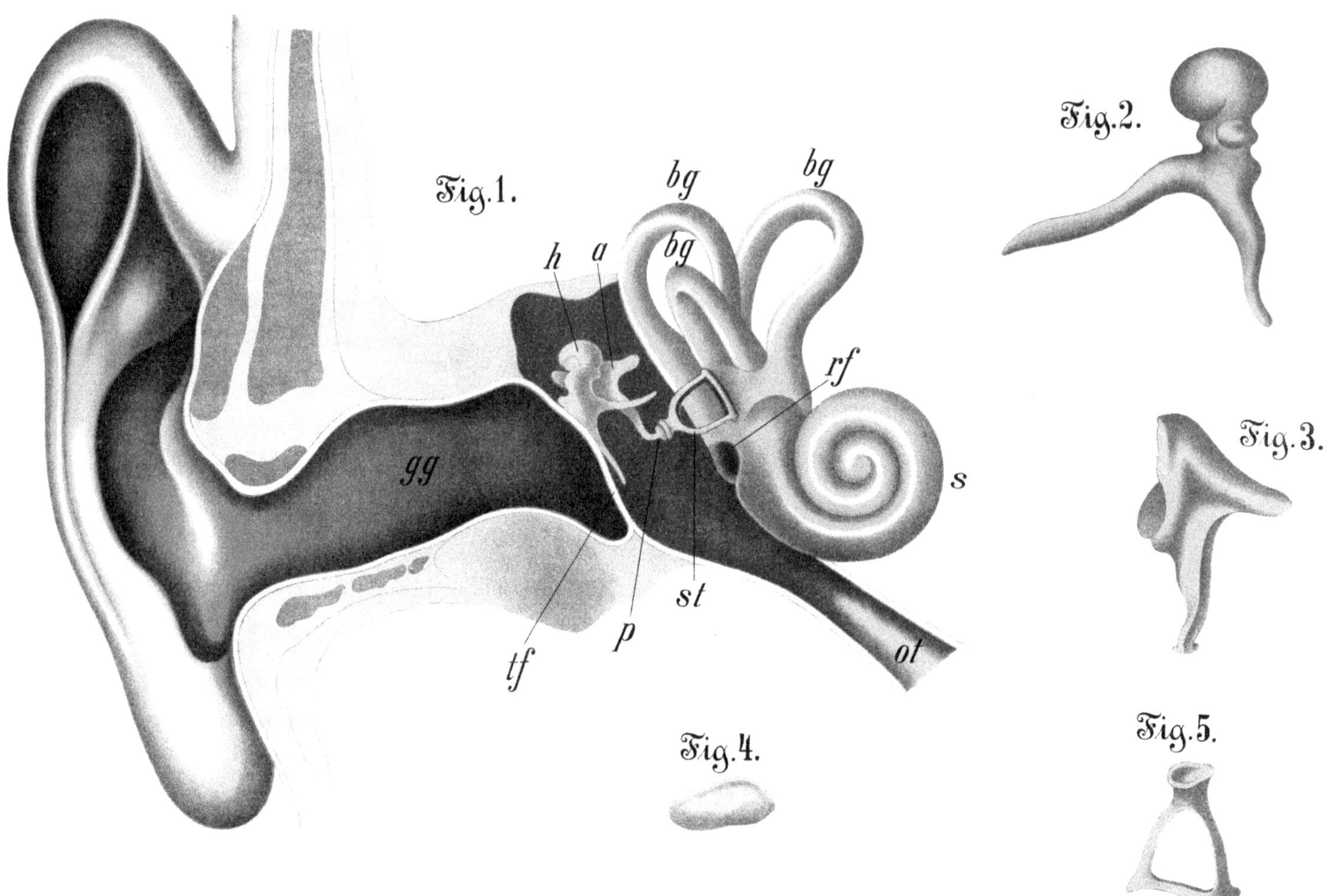

Artwork by R. Mendel

SCRATCH CONTINUED, FROM LAST PAGE

one of these lulls in sound, he thought he heard the scratching again.

Is that possible? Could I hear it all the way in the living room from my own room? IT can't be that loud?

He muted the TV. Nothing. He had to be sure. He went down the hallway, back to his room.

SCRATCH. SCRATCH. SCRATCH. Alvin screamed in frustration and kicked the wall.

"GET OUT! GET OUT! GET OUT! OR I'M GOING TO COME IN THERE AFTER YOU!"

Merciful silence.

Alvin turned to his bed. His warm, soft bed. He wanted to collapse into it and sleep till noon—

SCRATCH. SCRATCH. SCRATCH.

It wasn't going to stop. Alvin had no choice. He grabbed his sheets, a pillow, and went back to the living room. He set up on the couch, turned the TV to one of those weird all music stations, and tried to put the scratching sound out of his head. The sofa wasn't very comfortable, but it would have to do. There was no guest room, and Eric kept the master bedroom locked. It was the sofa or nothing. Alvin did his best to get comfortable.

He never really did.

He managed some sleep, but it was restless, and he woke up with a pain in his shoulder.

The first thing he did was check the outside wall. There were now two holes at the base of the wall that weren't there before. Alvin was confused, but now, he had a plan. He took the poison, spread the pellets around the holes, and for good measure along the wall. A dead animal in the wall wouldn't be any fun, but at least he'd know the problem was solved. Alvin went back inside, back to his room, back to his computer. His sanctuary. He heard the scratching that afternoon. Whatever was in the wall could scratch all day long. As long as it took the poison bait and died.

As night approached, Alvin grew nervous. The poison was supposed to be fast-acting. If whatever was in the wall had taken the bait, it should be dead by now. No more scratching. No more sleeping on the sofa.

But what if the poison doesn't work? What

SCRATCH CONTINUED, NEXT PAGE...

Artwork by Karl Wiener

SCRATCH CONTINUED, FROM LAST PAGE

if this thing in the walls doesn't go away? Will I ever sleep again?

Alvin pushed such thoughts out of his mind. He'd drive himself crazy if he kept this up. The scratching continued off, and on the rest of the night. Alvin checked the outside. The holes were still there. So were the poison pellets –all of them.

Or were they?

Maybe some of them were gone. Alvin had laid out so many it was hard to tell. He banged the shovel against the wall, which quieted the noise, but only for a little while. Alvin faced another night on the sofa. "No! This is my room, and I'm not going to let some rodent drive me out," Alvin said to the empty room. He came up with a new plan.

Alvin pushed his computer's subwoofer speaker up against the wall where the scratching was coming from and dropped the bass. He blasted the wall with the most bass-heavy dubstep he could find and cranked up the volume until he could feel the vibration in the wall and the floor. This was either going to drive the beasts away or cause a rave to break out in his walls. Alvin killed the lights, left his room, and let the dubstep blast for the next hour. He expected an angry call from the neighbors about the loud music, but it never happened. He passed the time in the living room watching TV and trying not to think of what his next step would be if this didn't work.

It was the moment of truth. Alvin went back to his room and turned off the music. No scratching. He waited a few minutes. Nothing. Alvin breathed a sigh of relief. He lowered the volume and put on some soft, mood music. The kind of stuff you'd hear in a spa and claimed it could realign your chakras or open your third eye. Alvin didn't care about that; he just wanted something he could ignore. He let the music play as he got ready for bed. He thought about turning it off but decided to let it keep going.

Maybe it will help me sleep?

It did help Alvin sleep. But, he couldn't stay asleep. He kept waking up and turning to the wall where he'd heard the scratching. He kept waiting for it to return. He knew it would return.

SCRATCH CONTINUED, NEXT PAGE...

Art by Paul Klee

SCRATCH CONTINUED, FROM LAST PAGE

Is that the sound? Is that them scratching, or is that just part of the music?

He passed the whole night like that and woke up exhausted. The music had stopped. Alvin got up to check his computer and possibly put on a new track—

SCRATCH. SCRATCH. SCRATCH.

"Soonest we could come out there would be a week from Friday," the man on the phone told Alvin.

"You've gotta be kidding. They're in the walls, man. Do you understand me? They are in my goddamn walls!"

"I understand sir. But we're swamped. Everyone is stuck at home and discovering just how many bugs and rodents live in their houses. Now, like I said. I can have someone come out there a week from Friday to make an inspection. Would you like to book that appointment?"

"Yes, yes, I would."

"Okay, then. If anything sooner opens up, we'll let you know."

Alvin ended the call and went to the backyard. The holes at the base of the wall were still there. As were the poison pellets. He'd kept an eye on the wall for most of the morning, hoping to see the beast reveal itself. It had yet to show, but he heard it a few times. He was sure of it. The sound was unmistakable now.

A week from Friday? How am I supposed to put up with this till then?! This is torture.

SCRATCH. SCRATCH. SCRATCHITY-SCRATCH—

Alvin grabbed the shovel and slammed it against the wall. He no longer cared about not damaging it. That was Eric's problem.

Eric? Lucky bastard! He's in nice quiet quarantine! He doesn't have to put up with this!

Alvin didn't stop banging until the shovel bent, which he was unaware shovels could do. He inspected the wall for damage, but it was spotless. Alvin chucked the shovel and rubbed his temples.

SCRATCH. SCRATCH. SCRATCH. SCRATCH.

He could feel the sound now. Feel it run through his body. However, the sound wasn't coming from the wall. It reverberated from his pocket. Alvin reached in and felt his buzzing phone. He answered, and it was the exterminator service.

"Hey, I'm glad I caught you. It turns out there's a technician in your area. He had a client cancel on him, so he's available. We can have him there in less than an hour."

SCRATCH CONTINUED, NEXT PAGE...

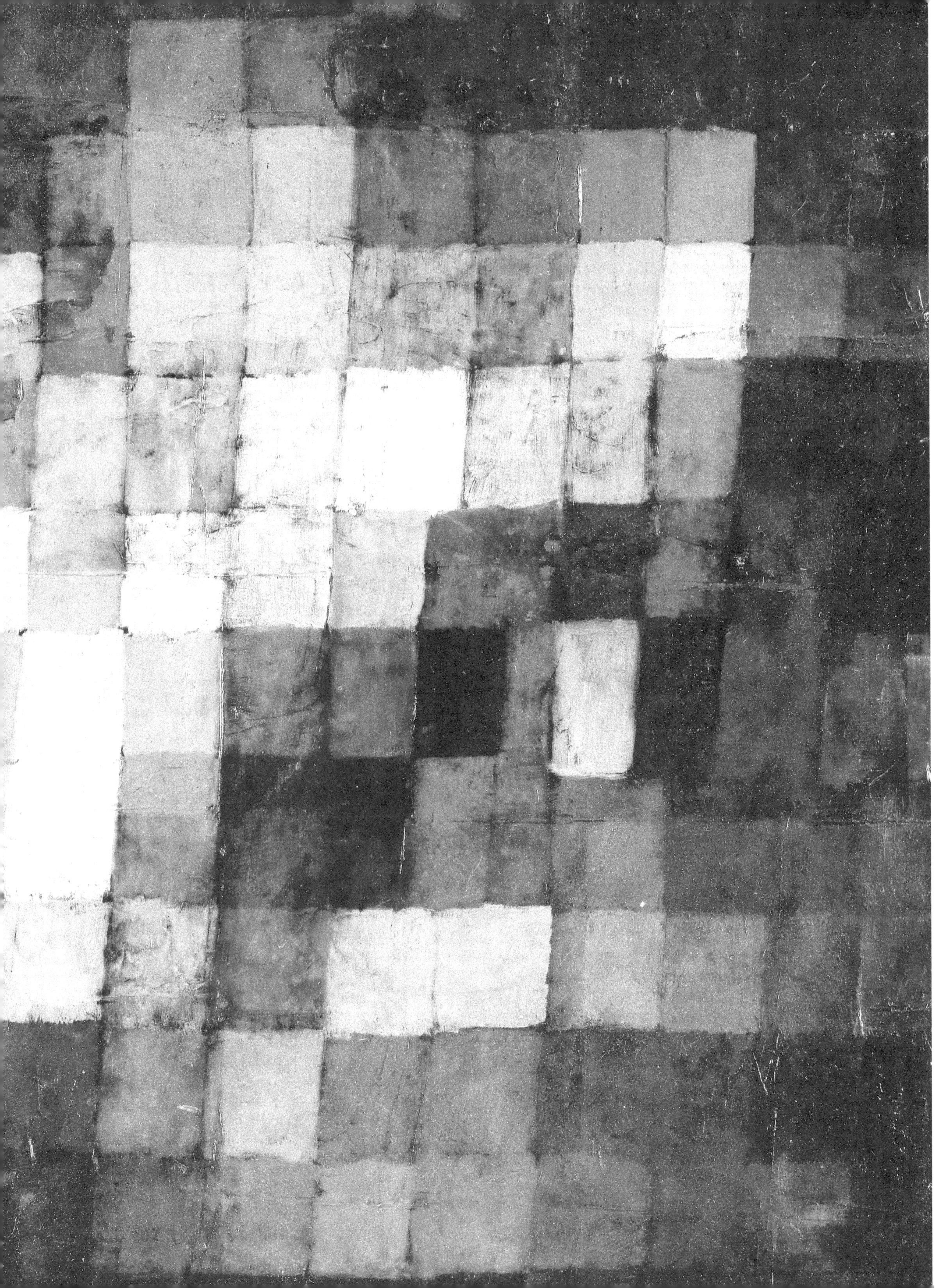

SCRATCH CONTINUED, FROM LAST PAGE

"Oh, my God. I LOVE YOU."

"They were there. I'm telling you they were right there. Two holes under the foundation," Alvin told the exterminator.

The holes were gone. The poison pellets were still there, right where the holes should have been.

"I'm telling you they were right there," Alvin said again.

The exterminator checked around the base of the wall and wrote something in his notebook.

"Even if the holes were still here, they might not have been the only point of entry. Rats and mice can flatten their bodies and squeeze through almost anything. If you're hearing the sound at night, it's probably rats. I'm going to check a few other things."

Alvin escorted the man around the house, into his bedroom, and even up to the attic. There were no holes, no droppings, nothing. Whatever was in the walls had left no trace of itself. More importantly, the scratching sound had stopped. Without evidence of an infestation, the exterminator told Alvin there was little he could do. He put out some traps and some more poison. He told Alvin he'd return a week from Friday at the previously scheduled time to see if there was anything more he could do. It wasn't the answer Alvin wanted to hear, but what choice did he have but to wait?
The house was quiet for the rest of the day.

At sunset, the scratching returned.

Nothing stopped it. Dubstep drowned it out, but as soon as Alvin turned it off.

SCRATCH. SCRATCH.

He kicked the wall on the inside.

SCRATCH. SCRATCH.

He hid out in the living room. Even with the TV on, he could hear the sound.

SCRATCH. SCRATCH. SCRATCH. SCRATCH.

It followed him from room to room. He'd have given anything to be able to check into a hotel room or an Air BnB. Anything to get away from the sound. But there was nowhere to go. Everything was closed because the country had shut down. He still had his car. He could sleep in there.

SCRATCH. SCRATCH. SCRATCH. SCRATCH.

It was impossible. Even in the car, he could hear it. Faint, like a draft through a tiny crack or the chirp of a cricket, caught on the wind.

SCRATCH. SCRATCH. SCRATCH.

Ignore it. It's nothing. It's not really there.

Alvin took a deep breath.

SCRATCH. SCRATCH. SCRATCH.

No, no, it's not real.

"There were no holes, no droppings, nothing. Whatever was in the walls had left no trace of itself. More importantly, the scratching sound had stopped."

SCRATCH. SCRATCH. SCRATCH.

Alvin opened the car door.

SCRATCH. SCRATCH. SCRATCH.

It was there somehow. Somehow it had followed him. No more poison. No more shovels. No more half measures. He rifled through the garage until he found what he was looking for –an aluminum baseball bat Eric had acquired at a garage sale. Alvin tested the weight. Perfect.

Am I really doing this?

SCRATCH. SCRATCH. SCRATCH.

Alvin ran toward the back of the house, bat in hand. He smashed the wall. Stucco and wood flew as the outside wall started to give in.

SCRATCH. SCRATCH. SCRATCH.

Alvin hit harder. Whack after whack. He woke a neighbor's dog. It barked along with every smash of the bat.

SCRATCH. SCRATCH. SCRATCH.

Alvin kept up the pressure. He had to get to it.

SCRATCH CONTINUED, NEXT PAGE...

Artwork by Karl Wiener

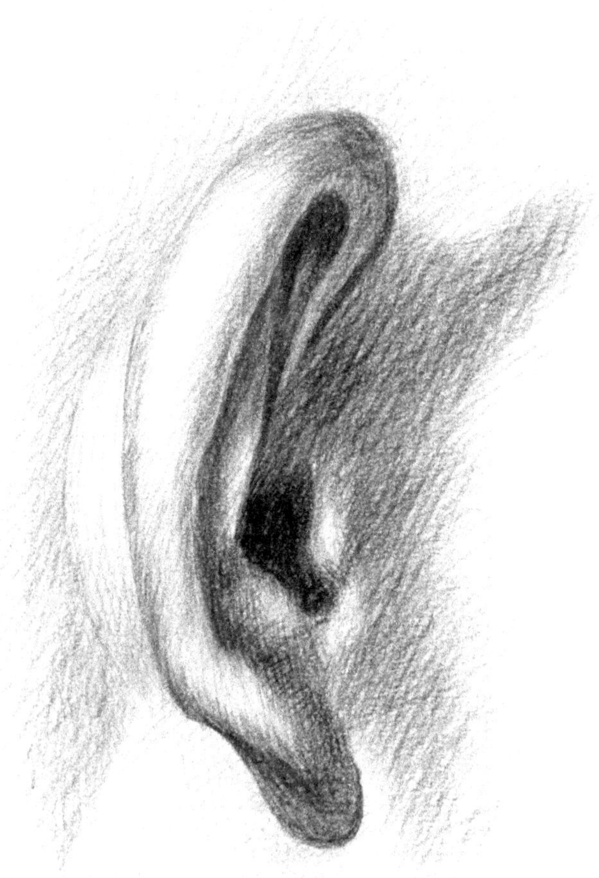

"He went inside, to his room, the original source. He listened for the noise."

(This page) Illustration by Richard Sanger Smith

Art by Karl Wiener (Opposite page)

SCRATCH CONTINUED, FROM LAST PAGE

Smash! Smash!

"Hey! What the hell's going on over there?!" someone shouted.

"It's nothing! Just taking care of a little rodent problem!" Alvin answered. "Come on out! Can't hide forever!"

The wall crumbled. Alvin shined his flashlight into the wreckage. Nothing. He went inside, to his room, the original source. He listened for the noise. "Come on. Come on. I know you're in there," Alvin said as he tapped the bat against the wall. For a moment, he dared to dream that he scared it away.

SCRATCH. SCRATCH. SCRATCH.

Alvin slammed the bat into the wall near his PC. Unlike the outside, the inside gave in on the first whack of the bat. He kept hammering away until the wall was almost gone. He admired his handy work, then looked into the hole. Nothing.

SCRATCH. SCRATCH. SCRATCH.

It was still there but in a different part of the wall. It had moved.

That's why I heard it in the garage. It's moving around the house!

He listened for it again. He wanted to make sure he hit the right spot.

SCRATCH. SCRATCH. SCRATCH.

He smashed the wall where he heard the sound. Nothing.

SCRATCH. SCRATCH. SCRATCH.

It was on the move. Alvin hit the wall again and again and again.

SCRATCH. SCRATCH. SCRATCH.

It was in the hallway. Alvin followed. He used the bat wherever he heard it.

SCRATCH. SCRATCH. SCRATCH.

Hallway.

SCRATCH. SCRATCH. SCRATCH.

Livingroom.

SCRATCH. SCRATCH. SCRATCH.

Now the floor of the living room.

SCRATCH. SCRATCH. SCRATCH.

Front hallway.

SCRATCH. SCRATCH. SCRATCH.

Master bedroom. He had to breakdown the door, but that didn't matter.

SCRATCH. SCRATCH. SCRATCH.

Back into the living room.

SCRATCH. SCRATCH. SCRATCH.

SCRATCH. SCRATCH. SCRATCH.

SCRATCH CONTINUED, NEXT PAGE...

SCRATCH CONTINUED, FROM LAST PAGE

SCRATCH. SCRATCH. SCRATCH.

SCRATCH. SCRATCH. SCRATCH.

Alvin dropped the bat. The sound. It was all around him, everywhere and nowhere at the same time.

SCRATCH. SCRATCH. SCRATCH.

There was only one explanation.

It's in my head. If it's not in the walls, or the floor, or in the house… it's in my head. I have to get it out of there.

Alvin went to the garage. He dug through Eric's stuff. If there was a tool for the job, Eric had it somewhere.

SCRATCH. SCRATCH. SCRATCH.

He found the power drill.

SCRATCH. SCRATCH. SCRATCH.

After a little more searching, he found the attachment he needed. A regular drill bit wouldn't do. He didn't need to go deep, he just needed to make a hole big enough for whatever was in there to crawl out.

SCRATCH. SCRATCH. SCRATCH.

He found it! The box of large circular, saw-toothed bits, the kind used to make cutouts in wood panels. He had to find the right sized bit. Large enough to let it out. Small enough to fit on his forehead. That was where he'd make the cut.

SCRATCH. SCRATCH. SCRATCH.

Alvin heard sirens, someone had called the cops. He found the right sized bit and went to the downstairs bathroom.

The police pounded on the door.

"POLICE! OPEN UP!"

He had to move fast. If the police came in and arrested him, they'd stop him. They'd never believe why he was doing it. They'd call him crazy and institutionalize him. This thing in his head would be stuck forever! He attached the drill bit, pulled the trigger, and the blade whirred to life. He looked at himself in the mirror.

Am I really doing this?

SCRATCH. SCRATCH. SCRATCH.

"What choice do I have?" Alvin said to himself.

The police kept pounding.

"WHOEVER IS IN THERE, OPEN THE DOOR NOW OR WE'RE GOING TO BREAK IT DOWN!"

It was now or never. Alvin lay on the tiled floor. He'd let gravity help him. He placed the saw-toothed bit against his forehead.

SCRATCH. SCRATCH. SCRATCH.

He heard the front door break.

SCRATCH. SCRATCH.

Alvin took a deep breath.

SCRATCH.

Pulled the trigger.

SCRA—

THE END

Artwork by Rudolf Bauer

THE VISITORS

by Ruben Quintana

"A blink broke the brief stillness and my panic turned to fear..."

Illustrations by Fitz

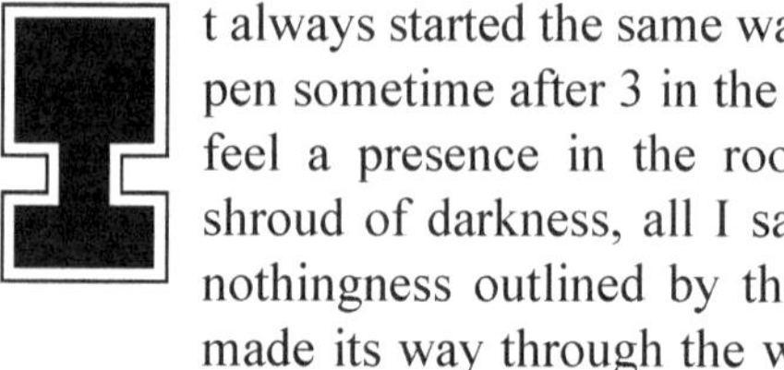

It always started the same way. It used to happen sometime after 3 in the morning. I could feel a presence in the room. Through the shroud of darkness, all I saw was the same nothingness outlined by the faint light that made its way through the window. My little brother would be in the bed perpendicular to mine and my younger brother right above mine in our bunk bed, both fast asleep.

Almost nightly, from the age of 13, I would awaken to an all too still room looming with the uneasiness that something is there, unseen and watching in the darkness.

The uneasiness suddenly was illuminated by a bright blue flash of light that would flood the room and what felt like a seizure would take hold of me. I'd instantly realize I couldn't move, the anxious desperation of being paralyzed turned into panic. A resonating sound like the humming of an electric transformer, or the low frequency buzzing of bees shook me to my core.

As I laid in bed paralyzed facing the inside of the room I noticed the outline of a figure. I began to focus on something in the darkness looking at me—it wasn't human. It stared through me with big dark glossy eyes. It had textured skin like a salamander, a dark and observant being, stared on as though observing an animal which made me feel uneasy.

A blink broke the brief stillness and my panic turned to fear as I tried to call out for my mom but no words would come out. I felt so helpless when I tried to speak. As fast as the onset of immobility took hold it always seemed to be on a count of three, like counting down before being put to sleep for surgery. It was always one, two, three and I only remember waking up in a panic.

That February was my first time I had experienced the visitations but it was not the last. It wasn't every day that I had these occurrences it was sporadic throughout my youth. I didn't see the entity every time. One time

was more than enough so I tried to keep my eyes closed after the first encounter but curiosity would get the best of me and I would get a glimpse of the shadows being cast on the wall of the movement in the room. At times it felt as though there were several of them in the room. I could feel their presence.

Eyes wide open or eyes wide shut every single time the blue light would fill the room a seizure-like state took hold and then I would blank out only to wake up

VISITORS CONTINUED, NEXT PAGE...

Art by Odilon Redon

"There would be instances of being placed in an alternate reality, in other places I had never seen, living temporary experiences that seemed all too real..."

VISITORS CONTINUED, FROM LAST PAGE

disoriented and every time in less of a panic.

Over time I had gotten accustomed to the visitations. I had rationalized that whatever was happening wasn't that bad because I would still be alive the next morning.

There were instances that didn't involve paralysis. There would be instances of being placed in an alternate reality, in other places I had never seen, living temporary experiences that seemed all too real, experiencing beautiful places I didn't want to wake up from.

Sometimes I would wake up from a dream, within a dream, within a dream. Keep in mind I'm the type of person that doesn't dream often. I go to sleep and then wake up rested but not having had some sort of dream.

As I got older, I coped with experiences and thought less about them as they stopped altogether. I couldn't let it go though; I read about sleep paralysis and sleeping disorders and where the answers to those topics didn't suffice.

Sometime decades later I happened to ask my younger brother at a family gathering if he had ever experienced the visitations at our old house. As I described the events and the details of having felt as if someone was in the room and the resonating sound similar to the humming of a transformer or the buzzing of bees and all of a sudden as I talked to my brother a blue flash of light flooded the room.

He stopped, tilted his head as though from a pain in the neck. All the family present dropped to the ground and couldn't move. The paralysis took control of the family. My mom, my wife, my kids, my brother and his kids and myself were all on the floor as though suffering from a seizure.

I laid facing up and three spindly, big headed, large eyed, with the textured skin as that of a salamander stood and looked at me as though observing an animal. The bigger one of the three waved his skinny long fingered hand in my face and I went blank. When I regained consciousness there was no one around me. Not my wife, my kids, my mom, my brother or any of his family. I was alone. That was the last time I saw my family again.

The End

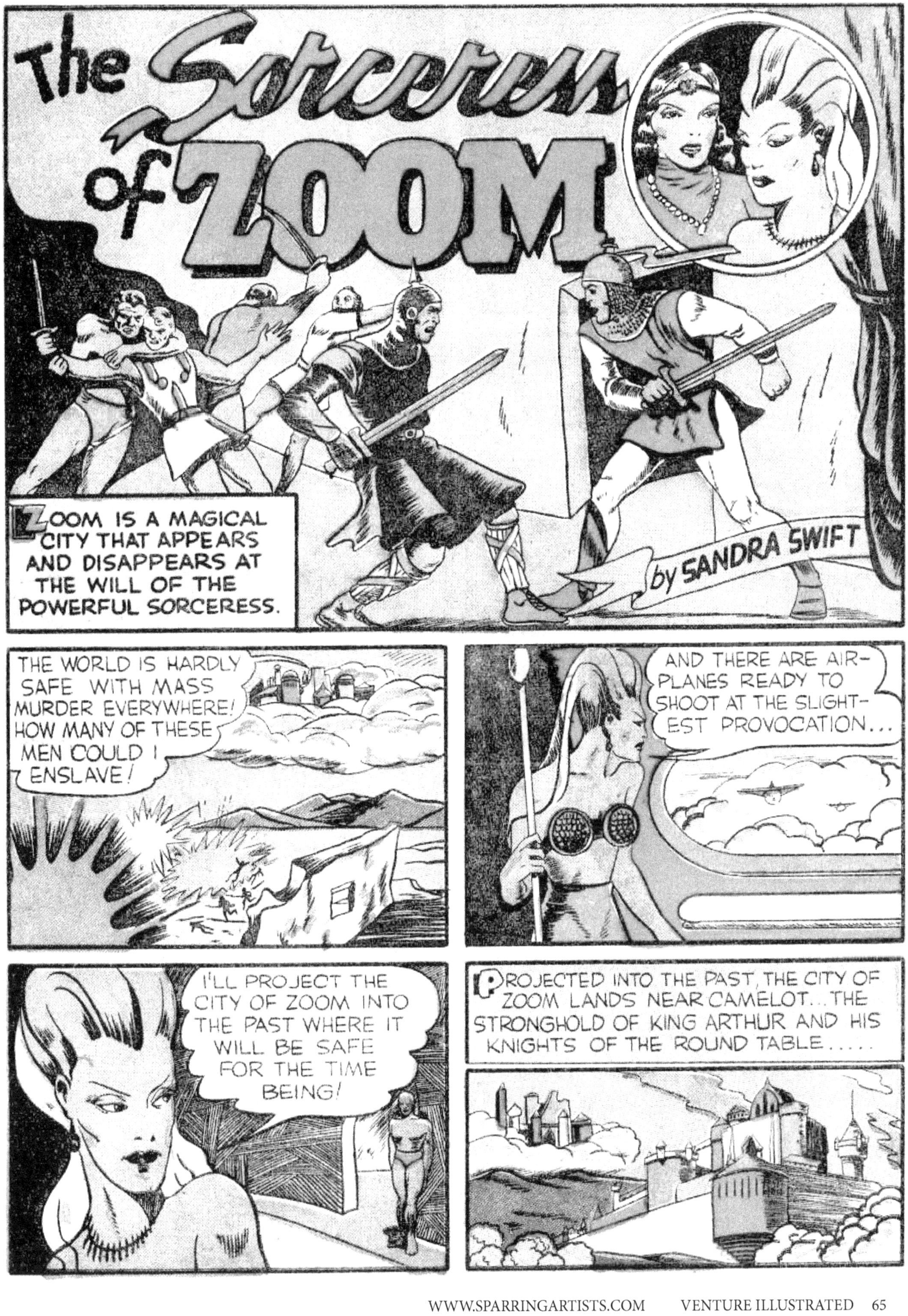

The Sorceress of ZOOM

ZOOM IS A MAGICAL CITY THAT APPEARS AND DISAPPEARS AT THE WILL OF THE POWERFUL SORCERESS.

by SANDRA SWIFT

PROJECTED INTO THE PAST, THE CITY OF ZOOM LANDS NEAR CAMELOT... THE STRONGHOLD OF KING ARTHUR AND HIS KNIGHTS OF THE ROUND TABLE.....

FOUR ROBBER BARONS AGAINST ONE KNIGHT! THEY DON'T SEEM TO BELIEVE IN FAIR PLAY!

THE LONE KNIGHT IS A BRAVE FELLOW...I'LL HELP HIM!

RELEASE MY FLYING DRAGON!

ZOUNDS! THIS KNIGHT IS A WIZARD!

MERLIN MUST HAVE SENT THIS DRAGON TO HELP ME!

HEAVENS! HE'S FAINTED! HIS WOUNDS MUST BE BAD!

WHY... IT'S SIR GARETH!

CARRY THIS NOBLE KNIGHT TO ZOOM, AND IF YOU VALUE YOUR LIVES...BE CAREFUL!
2

TRY TO DRINK THIS, SIR GARETH...IT WILL RESTORE YOUR STRENGTH!

IN SPITE OF THE LAVISH ATTENTION THE SORCERESS SHOWERS UPON HIM, SIR GARETH REMAINS DESPONDENT!
I WONDER WHAT MAKES HIM SO UNHAPPY... I'LL GET TO THE BOTTOM OF THIS!

THE SORCERESS CHANGES HER APPEARANCE TO THAT OF AN OLD HERMIT....
AS THE SORCERESS...SIR GARETH WILL NOT CONFIDE IN ME! BUT HOW CAN HE HELP BUT TRUST A WISE OLD MAN?

WHAT AILS THEE, SIR KNIGHT?

FATHER...THE UNSPEAKABLE SORCERESS QUEEN MORGANA LE FAY, KIDNAPPED MY DEMOISELLE, LADY ELAINE THE FAIR! AND I HAVE FAILED IN MY SWORN DUTY TO RESCUE HER!

STUNNED BY SIR GARETH'S TALE, THE SORCERESS IS OVERCOME BY TWO EMOTIONS.
I WISH I COULD HELP HIM...BUT I WANT HIM FOR MYSELF!

I HAVE IT! I'LL HELP QUEEN MORGANA GET RID OF LADY ELAINE! PERHAPS HE'LL APPRECIATE ME MORE AFTERWARDS!

ISMAL! COME HERE!
3

THAT ARMOR WILL PROTECT YOU FROM HARM!
NOW I SHALL RESCUE LADY ELAINE THE FAIR!

QUEEN MORGANA IS KING ARTHUR'S SISTER! HE DOESN'T WISH HER HARMED!
ISN'T THAT TOO BAD?

HOLD! NO KNIGHT CAN PASS THIS VALE WITHOUT FIGHTING ME!

WHOEVER YOU ARE... I'LL TRAMPLE YOU TO DUST!
EMPTY BOASTS-SIR KNIGHT!

THE TWO KNIGHTS COLLIDE WITH SUCH FORCE THEIR SPEARS BREAK!

YOU FIGHT LIKE A KNIGHT OF THE ROUND TABLE!
I AM!

OUR MASTER LORD IS IN DANGER! LET US ATTACK THIS WHITE KNIGHT!

MORE KNIGHTS! I MUSTN'T LET THEM HARM SIR GARETH!
4

HOW DO YOU LIKE THAT?

YIELD...SIR KNIGHT!

MERCY... I YIELD! WHO MIGHT YOU BE?
GO TO KING ARTHUR AND REPORT SIR GARETH SENT THEE!

CONGRATULATIONS FOR YOUR SPLENDID VICTORY, SIR GARETH!
HOW COULD A LADY FAIR KILL TWO STRONG KNIGHTS?

WHO WISHES TO HONOR THE CASTLE OF QUEEN MORGANA LE FAY?
THE QUEEN OF ZOOM AND SIR GARETH!

SIR GARETH AND THE QUEEN OF ZOOM REST IN THE GUESTS CHAMBERS, YOUR MAJESTY!
IF LADY ELAINE HEARS OF IT, SHE WILL KNOW HER KNIGHT CAME FOR HER!
I DECREE HER FOR MY SON, SIR MORDRED!

SLAY SIR GARETH!
IT SHALL BE DONE, YOUR MAJESTY!

THIS IS TO BE EXPECTED... QUEEN MORGANA IS A TREACHEROUS ONE!
5

THE SORCERESS COMMANDS THE CITY OF ZOOM TO SETTLE IN THE CASTLE!
TO MY AID... MY MEN!

TO OUR MISTRESS!
AEEE! YEEEGO!

YOU ASKED FOR IT... YOU JACKALS!

THIS WILL SAVE THE DAY FOR ME!

SO THAT'S YOUR GAME, IS IT? RELEASE MY FLYING DRAGONS!

WUHEEEEREOW!!

THE SORCERESS' HORDES WIN......
SURRENDER, OR WE'LL ANNIHILATE YOU!

WE YIELD!!
6

MY DRAGONS!
MY KNIGHTS!!
I'LL HAVE MY REVENGE!

I'LL CHANGE YOU INTO A PIG, SIR GARETH!
SO?

NOT YET, MY DEAR MORGANA! YOUR MAGIC IS PUNY COMPARED TO MINE!
THE SORCERESS COVERS SIR GARETH WITH A PROTECTIVE SCREEN...

CONFESS YOURSELF BEATEN!
YES! I AM BEATEN!

BUT I HAVE A TRUMP CARD TO PLAY! LADY ELAINE THE FAIR IS STILL MY CAPTIVE!

I WILL FIGHT SIR MORDRED FOR LADY ELAINE'S HAND!

NAY, SIR GARETH...I HAVE MY PLANS FOR LADY ELAINE!

COME... MY FLYING DRAGONS!
THIS IS IDEAL! I'LL MAKE SIR GARETH LOSE, AND ELAINE WEDS SIR MORDRED!
7

BE SURE NOT TO MISS THE FASCINATING ADVENTURES OF The SORCERESS of ZOOM IN THE NEXT ISSUE!

Illustration by Fitz

TEFILLAH'S ANSWER

BY NELSON GARY

Terence Kai Atlas and Kali Muladhara Sushumna once entertained controversial company in the Twilight Land's part of Lazareth, the scenic city of Card, with its mystic bascule bridge connecting it to Tantra Town lit up this sway of heart-minds soulfully enjoined as a singular beat in union with zigzagging brain waves in thingamajigs—conks—that often broke through enlightened by disciplined meditation on and felt prayer through mind-heavy, heartthrob Spirit in the wind as such and more. If a corpse was unclaimed after a month at Smashans, Kali's estate, it was reduced to debatably useless ashes or occasionally, though rarely, cooked and eaten while observing numerous rituals. It was a quandary for Atlas whether a corpse to be cremated could be put to use as furniture; then he remembered Buchenwald and a lampshade made of human skin found there. He was disgusted with himself for the thought even entering his mind as a spy on his soul. Postmortem cannibalism served to make Atlas more comfortable than he already was with his bodily mortality and more mindful of ways in which he could be compassionate to other living beings and please Kali, though he never altogether worshipped her the way he did Dr. Sophia Delphine Peoples, a world-famous forensic pathologist, who'd taken him as a barely legal, homeless whore—and a most excellent one—and given him an almost unending mission that still invigorated his life with meaning, even though he was disillusioned by what seemed to be the changeless verdict—that was until he met Kali.

She was the cosmic, headbanging heat that transformed unknown people's ashes into readable cosmic pulp. She supplied the energy of the cosmos to the pulp of

CONTINUED, NEXT PAGE...

Illustration by Thomas Nast

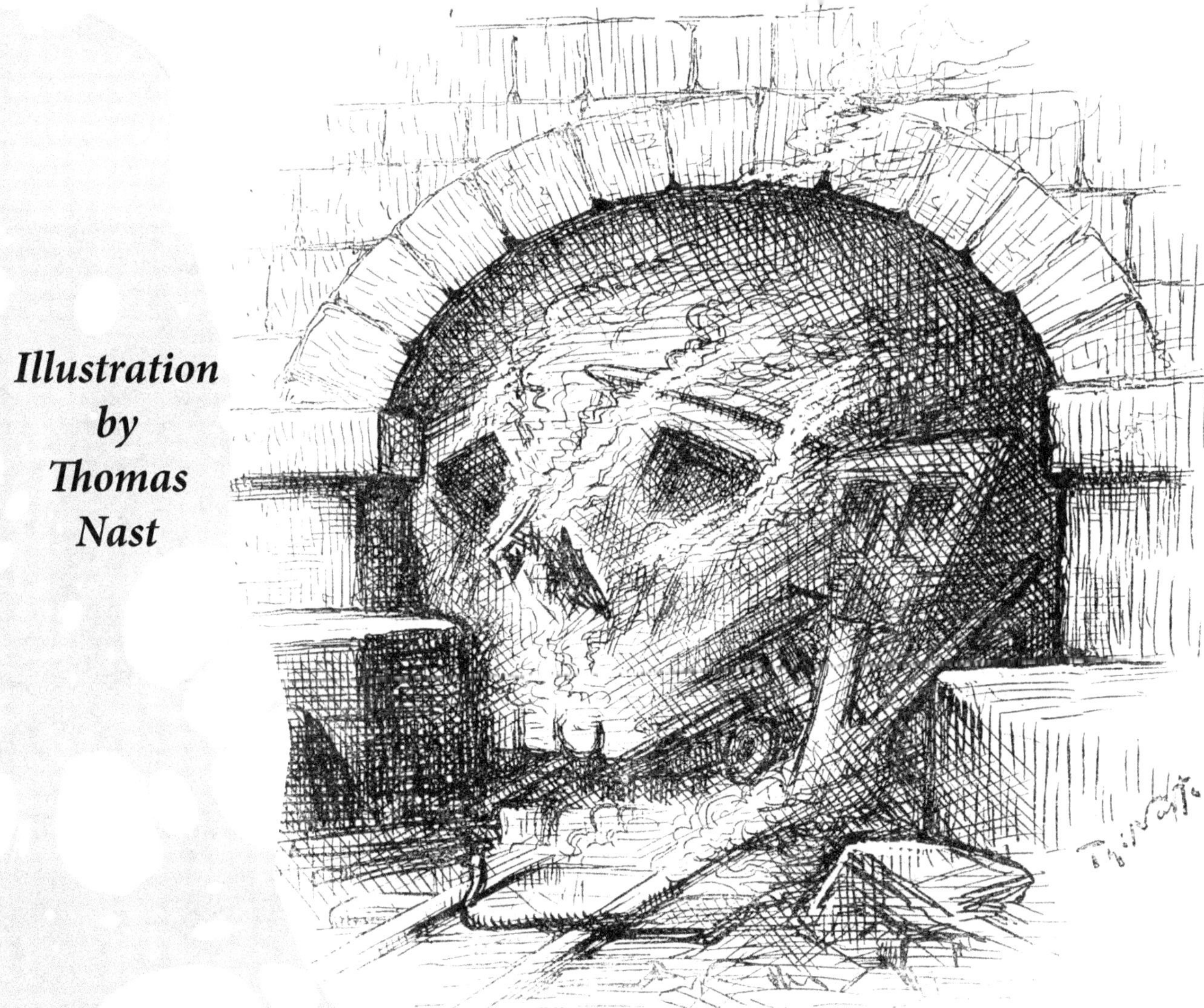

CONTINUED, FROM LAST PAGE

Atlas's muscular, somewhat stocky frame job. It often jibber-jabberwoke a poetic spiel about the politics of experience, about the permanence of soul in the impermanence of everything else, other than you bet your sweet ass, the Unknown God. Atlas constantly spouted, usually without sputtering, the psychospiritual geography he had acquired as part of his quest now ended. The man was more than a ripple of time; he was a stream that led into the river of the water of life with a gush, kissing Kali, Death, one time after the next after performing his mantras of mind and no-mind (mind without mind). When mind was without itself, the mind, an amalgamation, that collaborated with conditioning and social construction, there was the cosmic void, and the mind that remained was the mentality of the soul, which was nothing, not any one thing, therefore, infinite in possibility at once and later in potential.

One of the structural measures that kept those Lazareth conks organized was the rules of the conch, the *yoni*. Nobody knew this better than Twilight Terence with his history of prostitution and homicide. Most of both actions were done for the CIA—the five-finger discounts that Uncle Sam got on other countries, some with vulture debt, some not. Terry, what could one really say about him? He had juice, so it was natural that he had swagger. To say he was a full-blown mack daddy would be the God's truth. It was, however, a paradoxical pinch for him because he sought to transform power to neutral energy for everyone with their honored, respected duties, responsibilities, done towards love of, love for, and even love as part of the World Soul, Sophia. He could only begin to accomplish this goal with the help of Kali killing off a lot of him or, at least, a lot of who he'd come to believe he was. In Lazareth especially but in the Twilight Lands throughout, there was almost no law enforcement because there was no need for it.

CONTINUED, NEXT PAGE...

Illustration by Johannes Josephus Aarts

CONTINUED, FROM LAST PAGE

There was no need for it because cognitive organization and emotional regulation was self and nonself-monitored through a wise and desirous system by all its citizens, though their behavior was frequently unconventional because it was more spontaneous, thus more authentic than those conditioned largely unknowingly in the grand scheme of rings, cycles. Behavior indicated that which was observable, even oftentimes measurable; therefore, there were Sovereign Grand Inspectors. They accounted for this dimension of human experience as well as energy monitored on a cellular basis (living, dying, and dead cells).

They were essentially cops also tasked with energy conservation and pollution reduction. This work was connected with all of the above under the totality of the King of Lazareth's being. It was akin to the Godhead and had closer proximity to it than those on all planes of existence and nonexistence through largely his trains of thought when he was stationary in his *yogatantra (योगतन्त्र)*, his main "mode of meditation," reading and writing. Insightfully reading the thoughts and emotions of others as well as the related motives for their behaviors allowed him to write with such compassion and wisdom that his rule had been prosperous so far for him and his citizens without exception. Some Sovereign Grand Inspectors were also Lazareth Coincidence Control Operatives.

They served to make certain that synchronicity—particularly when Atomic Archetypes, psychoactive drugs, were taken—remained on plateaus of peak experiences without digressing into psychoses, unless psychoses were being experienced by trained clinicians or clinicians in training. It was illegal to treat psychoses, other than through medications, without firsthand experience of it in Lazareth and knowing Tantricity interventions for psychotic synchronicity, such as some restructuring methods known as Tantricide. The king had a settled mind, so when subjects acted out of accordance with his divine right to rule through *Hokhmah*, Wisdom, they were not punished, but they were brought into captivity to learn greater obedience to Christ.

Many Lazareth citizens, soulful, emotion-fueled thought forms, affectionately called the king "Chairperson Meow" because he sat in a chair, reading and writing, lovingly caring for his people and land, and he was the cat's meow in many ways, including his fondness for flappers, who evolved into ravers, specifically and the Roaring Twenties that he stopped to remember daily twenty times a day through his ritual pack of bones stuffed with tobacco marrow, coffin nails, which reached out to Christ coming with the clouds. The only thing that was known to roar with holy meaning in Lazareth was its ocean, the unconscious mind without mind of the king that became the mind of Christ, generating a significant amount of energy in the Holy Spirit's comforting waves on the shore and far and wide beyond to bodies, which were, as the ancient Greeks knew, infinitely penetrable. It was thought that one day the Revelation rumor, prophecy, would occur when the Lion of the tribe of Judah, which many of those in Lazareth twinned with another symbol, Durga's big cat, opened the seven seals, *mudras*, pointing to the seven churches, the seven chakras of the King of Lazareth, a scroll of a soul. He'd then become one with the Word but not as it. The Word would transform into another of his manifestations, the Lamb, the lamp of new Jerusalem, its sole container of light (the *Shekhinah* glory of God), a city which would require neither sun nor moon (eternal twilight).

The Kingdom Age probably wouldn't occur until the king's *jhator*, sky burial, a Tibetan Buddhist ritual of more violence than anything filmed in a "Bloody Sam"

CONTINUED, NEXT PAGE...

CONTINUED, FROM LAST PAGE

Peckinpah Western. In the ritual, the king's corpse would be placed at the top of Elijah Mountain, the highest peak in Lazareth, and pecked apart by vultures in tribute to his many friends devoted to this Tantric way of life, though the ruler's Tantra was of a different order. The sky burial would be the last funeral rite in a series of many honoring all the world's major faiths, a few of its cults as well as sex, spirituality, and rock 'n' rave. His Tibetan Buddhist brothers and sisters, even ones who weren't his subjects, would ritually enact the Bardo Thodol for 49 days with the butter lamp always representing Shekhinah in the lamp of the Lamb, the Apocalyptic Word, streaked with twilight, sacrificial blood; the king saw himself as nonattached in life and would remain so in death, a witness to what was and what wasn't.

When Atlas was in Kali during *maithuna*, twinning, ritual sexual intercourse, he was in the manger, that container called Death. She allowed him to experience the little death every 4-6 weeks, as followed and prescribed by many *Tantrikas*. As the manger, Kali held Jesus Christ born to die in order to cosmically deliver and liberate the world from karmic debts, the wages of sin, past, present, and future through him being sacrificed in ultraviolent blood, gore, and total debasement (in her eyes in more of her fullness as time and the devourer of time) to the ends of his divine and human ego death as legally decreed by the code and ordinance 666, which was *gevurah*, judgment at its most severe (the Stone Tablets of the Law were 6 by 6 by 6 handbreadths), with additional proto-Kabbalistic charges tacked on from the Babylonian exile in captivity. While there were epic narratives and concise vignettes about Atlas, what the world knew him least for was what he was most proficient in, and that was words: he had taken all words and the Word back to its source in nothing.

This prayer involved more actions than words, and it was called *tefillah*, the highest prayer in Kabbalah. One had to remove all obstacles that stood in the way of taking everything back to nothing. Atlas knew how he had removed some people, places, and things wasn't right. He had no doubt that he had taken everything that God spoke into existence back to the infinite nothingness of *Ayin*, but with this holistic prayer of mind, body, and soul in the Spirit, he had not received a blessing or a curse. He had received nothing, and as such he was deeply grieved until he met Kali, who told him: "You haven't taken everything back to nothing. You forgot one thing, yourself. You have to become Shiva, 'that which is not.' I can help you."

"Shiva means 'seven' in Hebrew. Shiva's a seven-day mourning period after a funeral."

"I don't know that the ego is anything to mourn."

Kali was even more terrifying than Atlas, so he knew he had something to learn from her, but beyond the teacher-student relationship, he was in love with Kali and she with him. She even let him wear her *Mundamala*, a garland of skulls, at home where both of them were always skyclad, naked. The skulls were evidence of Kali's power over life, death, and afterlife scenarios, theoretical and practical. What was most important to him was that the skulls represented one of the alphabets he had returned to nothing: Sanskrit. He regularly told Kali of his accomplishment with the substance of communication and that which it represented in letters. The skulls of hers contained infinite knowledge. Finally, Kali stated, "I said this, and I did that. I've cared as compassionately as I can about this matter that's eating you up. You're naked!"

"So are you!" Atlas shouted.

"But I know better. The ego, the I-maker, is one layer of the robe of the soul. The one you don't need. I don't need you.

CONTINUED, NEXT PAGE...

Illustration by Odilon Redon

"There's no blacker operation than me, government, military, alchemical, or other. You're coming closer to the ultimate reality with your increasing, experiential, felt awareness of billions of your cells..."

Artwork by Ara Azul (Opposite page)

CONTINUED, FROM LAST PAGE

And if you don't need me, A-OK, but if that's the case, just split like yesterday."

"Why don't you need me?"

"I'm Death with a capital 'D,' Atlas."

"*Maveth*," he muttered.

Kali continued, "Ha! There are others, baby. I'm omnipresent in life. Every being's beginning is born with its end. Watch yerself, Atlas!"

"I'd rather watch you."

"Once a spy always a spy."

"Kali, 'She Who Is Black.'"

"There's no blacker operation than me, government, military, alchemical, or other. You're coming closer to the ultimate reality with your increasing, experiential, felt awareness of billions of your cells, the building blocks of your life, dying each day while you breathe the omnipresent air, the breath of God, the Holy Spirit, in my presence, which makes that air rarefied. So, G-d did nothing for everything you did for Him. You're here, aintchya? I mean, who cares, man?! I'm tired of hearing you sing the blues about nothing, your ego. Look, you definitely haven't abided by *Dharma* a lotta the time, and you've broken practically every commandment in the Holy Bible! So, you returned every word and the Word Himself back to their source in nothing, and you got nothing for it."

"That's fuckin' right! Not a fuckin' thing!"

"Other than a new understanding of yourself and everything else. Getting nothing is being given grace. And it's a big-time blessing!"

"How so?!"

"Because you became nothing, allowing yourself to become a microcosm of all creation, preservation, and destruction. Truthfully, if you hadn't done that and for the better part stayed that way, I'd never have given you the time of twilight. Never! You can keep your mind on and take it off with no-mind to experience that part of the World Soul, Wisdom, that's your soul whom I'm sharing my digs with, but take your ego out once and for all and leave it as one of the myriad other ego doormats outside the doors of my place."

Kali's doormat, Shiva, Bhairava, with her right foot now on his chest, never prayed in public, as was prescribed by the New Testament, but those who knew him knew well of his tefillah practice in its generalities, that it existed. It was now finally completed. His prayer had been answered.

The End

GROVE OF THE UNBORN

by LYN VENABLE

Illustration by HANNES BOK

"He thought of the ship, a silver streak now...

Grove of the Unborn

by Lynn Venable

Tyndall heard the rockets begin to roar, and it seemed as though the very blood in his veins pulsated with the surging of those mighty jets. Going? They couldn't be going. Not yet. Not without him! And he heard the roaring rise to a mighty crescendo, and he felt the trembling of the ground beneath the room in which he lay, and then the great sound grew less, and grew dim, and finally dissipated in a thin hum that dwindled finally into silence. They were gone.

Tyndall threw himself face down on his couch, the feel of the slick, strange fabric cold and unfriendly against his face. He lay there for a long time, not moving. Tyndall's thoughts during those hours were of very fundamental things, that beneath him, beneath the structure of the building in which he was confined, lay a world that was not Earth, circling a sun that was not Sol, and that the ship had gone and would never come back. He was alone, abandoned. He thought of the ship, a silver streak now in the implacable blackness of space, threading its way homeward through the stars to Sol, to Earth. The utter desolation which swept over him at the impact of his aloneness was more than he could endure, and he forced himself to think of something else.

Why was he here then? John Tyndall, 3rd Engineer of the starship Polaris. It had been such a routine trip, ferrying a group of zoologists and biologists around the galaxy looking for unclassified life-supporting planets. They had found such a world circling an obscure sun half way across the galaxy. An ideal world for research expedition, teeming with life, the scientists were delighted. In a few short months they discovered and cataloged over a thousand varieties of flora and fauna peculiar to this planet, called Arrill, after the native name which sounded something like Ahhrhell.

CONTINUED, NEXT PAGE...

...in the implacable blackness of space..."

Illustration by HANNES BOK

GROVE CONTINUED, FROM LAST PAGE

Yes, there were natives, humanoid, civilized and gracious. They had seemed to welcome the strangers, as a matter of fact they had seemed to expect them.

The Arrillians had learned English easily, its basic sounds not being too alien to their own tongue. They had quite a city there on the edge of the jungle, although, in circling the planet before landing, the expedition had noted that this was the only city. On a world only a little smaller than Earth, one city, surrounded completely by the tropical jungle which covered the rest of the world. A city without power, without machinery of any kind, and yet a city that was self-sufficient.

Well-tilled fields stretched to the very edge of the jungle, where high walls kept out the voracious growth. The fields fed the city well, and clothed it well. And there were mines to yield up fine metal and precious gems. The Earthmen had marveled, and yet, it had seemed strange. On all this planet, just one city with perhaps half a million people within its walls. But this was not a problem for the expedition.

The crew of the Polaris and the members of the expedition had spent many an enjoyable evening in the dining hall of the palace-like home of the Rhal, who was something more than a mayor and something less than a king. Actually, Arrill seemed to get along with a minimum of government. All in all, the Earthmen had summed up the Arrillians as being a naive, mild, and courteous people. They probably still thought so, all of them, that is, except Tyndall.

Of course, now that he looked back upon it, there has been a few things ... that business about the Bugs, as the Earthmen had dubbed the oddly ugly creatures who seemed to occupy something of the position of a sacred cow in the Arrillian scheme of things. The Bugs came in all sizes, that is all sizes from a foot or so in length up to the size of a full human.

CONTINUED, NEXT PAGE...

"The Time had been something else again, bringing with it, the first sign of real Arrillian fanaticism and the first hint of violence."

GROVE CONTINUED, FROM LAST PAGE

The Bugs were not permitted to roam the streets and market places, like the sacred cows of the Earthly Hindus. The Bugs were kept in huge pens, which none but a few high-ranking priests were permitted to enter, and although the Earthmen were not prevented from standing outside the pens and watching the ugly beasts munching grass or basking in the sun, the Arrillians always seemed nervous when the strangers were about the pens. The Earthmen had shrugged and reflected that religion was a complexity difficult enough at home, needless to probe too deeply into the Arrillian.

But The Time had been something else again, bringing with it, the first sign of real Arrillian fanaticism and the first hint of violence. Tyndall and four companions were strolling in a downtown section of the city, when all at once a hoarse cry in Arrillian shattered the quiet hum of street activity.

"What did he say?" asked one of Tyndall's companions, who had not learned much Arrillian.
"I—I think, 'A Time! A Time!' What could ..." he never finished the sentence, all about them Arrillians had prostrated themselves in the rather dirty street, covering their faces with their hands, lying face down. The Earthmen hesitated a moment, and a priest of Arrill appeared as though from nowhere, a wicked scimitar-like weapon in his hand and a face tense with anger.

"Dare you," he hissed in Arrillian, "dare you not hide your eyes at A Time!" He pushed one of the Earthmen with surprising strength, and the latter stumbled to his knees. All five men hastened to ape the position of the prostrate Arrillians; they knew better to risk committing sacrilege on a strange planet. As Tyndall sank to the ground and covered his eyes, he heard that priest mutter another sentence, in which his own name was included. He thought it was "You, Tyn-Dall ... even you."

A few moments later a bell sounded from somewhere, and the buzzing of conversation began around them, along with the shuffling, scraping sound of many people getting to their feet at once. A hand

CONTINUED, NEXT PAGE...

"...they were interested neither in the Arrillians, their offspring nor their religion, but merely in the flora and fauna of the planet, both of which seemed to be rather deadly."

GROVE CONTINUED, FROM LAST PAGE

touched Tyndall's shoulder and an Arrillian voice, laughing now, purred, "Up stranger, up, The Time is past."

The Earthmen got to their feet. Everything about them was the same as though nothing had happened, people strolling along the street, going in and out of shops, stopping to chat.

"I guess that was the all-clear," commented one wryly.

The others laughed nervously, but Tyndall was strangely troubled, he was thinking of the strange words of the priest, "You, Tyn-Dall, even you." Why should he have known, and not the others? He tried to forget it. Arrillian was a complex tongue with confusing syntax, perhaps the priest had said something else. But Tyndall knew one thing for certain, the mention of his name had been unmistakable.

The mood hung on, and quite suddenly Tyndall had asked, "I wonder about the children. Why do you suppose it is?"

One of the men laughed, "Maybe they feed them to the Bugs." At no time, during their stay on Arrill, had they seen a single child, or young person under the age of about twenty-one. The crew had speculated upon this at great length, coming to the conclusion that the youngsters were kept secluded for some reason known only to the Arrillians, probably some part of their religion. One of them had made so bold as to ask one of the scientists who politely told him that since his group was not composed of ethnologists or theologists, but of biologists and zoologists, they were interested neither in the Arrillians, their offspring nor their religion, but merely in the flora and fauna of the planet, both of which seemed to be rather deadly. The expedition had had several close calls in the jungle, and some of the plants seemed as violently carnivorous as the animals.

It was just a few days after the incident that the Arrillians kidnapped Tyndall. It had been a simple, old-fashioned sort of job, pulled off with efficiency and

CONTINUED, NEXT PAGE...

"It happened suddenly and silently, the hand clapped over his mouth, the forearm constricting his windpipe, his legs jerked out from under him, and a rag smelling sickly-sweet shoved under his nose, bringing oblivion..."

Illustration by HANNES BOK

GROVE CONTINUED, FROM LAST PAGE

dispatch as he wandered a few hundred feet away from the ship. It was late, and he had been unable to sleep, so he had strolled out for a smoke. The nightwatch must have been somewhere about on patrol, probably only a few hundred feet away, on the other side of the ship. It happened suddenly and silently, the hand clapped over his mouth, the forearm constricting his windpipe, his legs jerked out from under him, and a rag smelling sickly-sweet shoved under his nose, bringing oblivion.

When he came to consciousness, he found himself in this room, and he knew that since then, many days and nights had passed. His wants were meticulously attended to, his bath prepared, his food brought to him regularly, delicious and steaming, with a generous supply of full-bodied Arrillian wine to wash it down. Fresh clothes were brought to him daily, the loose-flowing, highly ornamented robe of the Arrillian noble. Tyndall knew he was no ordinary prisoner, and somehow, this fact made him doubly uneasy.

And then, tonight, the ship had blasted off without him. Tyndall could easily reconstruct what had happened when his crewmates had inquired about him, at the palace and in town. "Tyn-Dall?" Then, a sorrowful expression, a shrugging of the shoulders, a pointing toward the death-infested jungle, and a mournful shaking of the head, sign language which in any tongue meant, "Tyn-Dall wanders too far from your ship. He becomes lost. Alas, he does not know our jungle and its perils." Those who spoke a little English would make some expression of sympathy.

Maybe the crew was a little suspicious, maybe they thought there was something fishy about the thing, and then they thought of the unhappy results of what was commonly referred to as an "interplanetary incident." Ever since the people of the second planet of Alpha Centauri, in the early days of extraterrestrial exploration, had massacred an entire expedition because the captain had mortally insulted a tribal leader by re-

CONTINUED, NEXT PAGE...

Artwork by FRANK R. PAUL

GROVE CONTINUED, FROM LAST PAGE

fusing a sacred fruit, such incidents had been avoided at all costs.

And so, they dared not offend the Arrillians by questioning the veracity of their statements. And the jungle was deadly, so they looked a little longer, and asked a few more questions. After a little while, the scientists had completed their work and were anxious to get home, and so, the ship blasted off, without him.

All this had passed kaleidoscopically in Tyndall's mind as he lay on the couch in his luxurious prison, too numb to weep or even curse. His reverie was broken by the clicking of the lock and he raised up to see the door opening. An Arrillian servant stood there, his silver hair done up in the complicated style which denoted male house servants. He was unarmed. The houseman smiled, roared in imitation of a rocket, made a swooping gesture with one hand to indicate the departing ship, then pointed at Tyndall and at the open door. The servant bowed and departed, leaving the door slightly ajar. Now that the ship was gone, he was free to leave his room.

Tyndall stepped cautiously out of the room and found himself in a long hall, with many doors opening

CONTINUED, NEXT PAGE...

Illustration by Paul Orban

GROVE CONTINUED, FROM LAST PAGE

from it on either side, much like a hotel corridor. One end of the hall seemed to open out onto a garden and he started in that direction.

The doorway opened out into a patio which overlooked a vast and perfectly tended garden. The verdant perfection of the scene was marred only by one of the Bugs, sunning itself and gnawing on the stem of a flower. Tyndall was impressed again with the repulsive ugliness of the thing. This one was the size of a small adult human, and even vaguely human in outline, although the brownish armored body was still more suggestive of a big bug than anything else known to him. There were even rudimentary wings furled close to the curving back, and the underside was a dirty, striped gray. Tyndall shuddered, wondering why the Arrillians, who so loved to surround themselves with beauty, should choose so horrendous a creature as the object of their worship, or protection.

He heard running footsteps behind him, and turned to see the Arrillian houseman, breathless, with an expression of greatest concern on his face. The servant bowed respectfully before Tyndall, then gestured at the garden, shook his head vigorously from side to side and tugged at the Earthman's sleeve.

"Forbidden territory, eh? Okay, old fellow, what now?"

The servant motioned for Tyndall to follow him, and ushered him down the hall from whence he had just come, and into another of the rooms opening off from it. The very old man reclining upon the low, Roman-like couch, Tyndall recognized at once as his host, the Rhal of Arrill.

The Rhal touched the fingertips of both hands to his forehead in the Arrillian gesture of greeting, and Tyndall did the same. He noticed several male Arrillians standing near the back of the room, although the servant had bowed and retired.

"Well, Tyn-Dall, how do you enjoy the hospitality of Ahhreel?" He, of course, gave the native pronunciation to the name which was almost Teutonic in sound and unpronounceable for Tyndall because of the sound given to the double aspirate, for which he knew no equivalent.

"Your English, Dheb Rhal, has improved greatly since our last meeting," commented Tyndall guardedly, using the Arrillian prefix of extreme respect.

The old man smiled. "Your friends were kind enough to lend me books and also the little grooved disks that make voice." He gestured toward an old-fashioned wind-up type phonograph which Tyndall recognized at once as being standard aboard interstellar vessels, and for just such a purpose. The Rhal continued, "For teaching English very fine. How are you enjoying our hospitality, I ask again?"

Tyndall was stuck on Arrill and he knew it. There was no need to cook his own goose by being deliberately offensive. "I appreciate the hospitality of Arrill, I express my thanks for

CONTINUED, NEXT PAGE...

GROVE CONTINUED, FROM LAST PAGE

the consideration of my hosts but—if I may ask a question?"

"Yes?"

"What, in the wisdom of the Dheb Rhal, is the reason for my—er—detainment?"

"To answer that, Tyn-Dall, I must tell you something of the past of Ahhreel, and of her destiny." At these words, the other Arrillians in the room drew closer, and the Rhal motioned them to a couch at his feet and nodded toward Tyndall, requesting that he join them. Tyndall noticed that the others were gazing up into the old man's face with an expression of raptness, even of reverence. He knew that the Rhal did not possess an especially exalted position politically, even though he was head of the city. He guessed therefore that the Rhal must be the religious ruler of Arrill as well.

The Rhal began, intoning the words as though he were reciting a ritual, "There was a time, many thousands of Khreelas ago, when the kingdom of Ahhreel was not one small city, as you see it now, but a mighty empire, girdling the world in her vastness. But the people of Ahhreel had become evil in their ways, and her cities were black with sin. It was then that Xheev himself left his kingdom in paradise and appeared to the people of Ahhreel, and he told them that he was displeased, and that bad times would fall upon Ahhreel, and that her people would dwindle in number, and became exceedingly few, and the jungle would reclaim her emptied cities. One city, and only one, would survive and prosper, and the people of that city would be given the chance to redeem Ahhreel, and remove the heavy hand of Xheev's terrible punishment.

"All this came to pass, and in the dark Khreelas that followed, all of Ahhreel vanished except this city. Now, for many, many thousands of Khreelas, the people of this city have striven to redeem Ahhreel by obeying the sacred laws of Xheev.

"Xheev had promised that when the punishment was ended, he would send a sign, and his sign would be that a great silver shell should fall from the heavens, and within would be Xheev's own emissary, who must wed the ranking priestess of Xheev, establishing again the rapport between the kingdom of paradise and the world of Ahhreel."

When the Rhal had finished, the other Arrillians in the room fastened the same look of reverence upon Tyndall which they had formerly reserved for the Rhal.

Illustration by Jerry Kamstra

CONTINUED, NEXT PAGE...

"That is why we had to use ... devious means to make certain that your companions would not prevent the fulfillment of the prophesy."

GROVE CONTINUED, FROM LAST PAGE

Tyndall chose his words carefully. "But there were many aboard my vessel. Why did you, Dheb Rhal, select me as the emissary of Xheev?"

"Xheev selected you, I recognized you, as of all your companions, you and you alone have the sun-colored hair, which is the sacred color of Xheev."

Tyndall was able to question the Rhal almost coolly, the trap was already sprung, the ship was gone. Now, he only wanted to know the how, and the why. An accident of pigmentation, only that had brought him to this. Sun-colored hair!

"But, Dheb Rhal, did my friends and I not often tell you of ourselves, of the place from which we came? A world, a world like your own?"

The old man smiled. "Do not think me naive, Tyn-Dall. I am quite aware that you are but a man, a man from another world, although quite an incredible world it must be. I know also that you were, until this hour, unaware of your destiny. I knew that when my priest reported that you ignored the Ritual Of The Time, until literally forced to obey. That is why we had to use ... devious means to make certain that your companions would not prevent the fulfillment of the prophesy. Now, of course, you understand.

"I do not think the priestess Lhyreesa will make you unhappy, Tyn-Dall."

This was not Earth and these people were not Earthmen. The thought now did not bring the bitter pain it had at first, right after the ship left. Earth already was becoming hazy in Tyndall's mind, a lovely globe of green somewhere ... somewhere far, and home once, a long time ago.

No, the Arrillians were not Earthmen, but they were human, and an attractive, gracious race. Life would not be bad, among the Arrillians, especially as the espoused of the ranking priestess of Arrill. Tyndall fingered the rich material of his Arrillian robe; he thought of the food, the wine, the servants. No, he decided, not bad at all. One thing, though—this priestess Lhyreesa ...

"I have, then, but one request to make, Dheb Rhal, I would like to see the priestess Lhyreesa."

The old man almost chuckled, "That is understandable, Tyn-Dall, but it is not yet The Time."

Tyndall, reveling in the strength of his position, grew bolder. "I would like very much, Dheb Rhal, to see her now."

The Rhal's face darkened. "Very well, Tyn-Dall, but I warn you, do not enter the Grove. There is death there, death that even I am powerless to prevent. The Guardians will not harm her, but any stranger ... will not live many minutes in the Grove."

"I will not enter, Dheb Rhal."

"Tyn-Dall, The Time is very soon, possibly this very hour. Will you not wait?"

"I prefer not to wait, Dheb Rhal."

The Rhal gestured to a young Arrillian. "Bheel, show Tyn-Dall to the Grove of the priestess Lhyreesa."

The younger man protested, "But, Dheb Rhal, so near The Time, what if ..."

"Do as I command," snapped the Rhal.

Bheel turned silently, motioning for Tyndall to follow. The young Arrillian led Tyndall the length of the corridor, back to the patio he had stepped onto by mistake earlier in the day. Bheel stepped respectfully aside. Tyndall looked out into the garden. The sun was beginning to set, the long shadows stretched across the dim recesses of tropic greenery. The huge insect-like thing was still there, stretched out in a narrow strip of sunlight, catching the last failing waves of warmth from the sinking sun.

Tyndall turned to the Arrillian. "Where might I find the priestess Lhyreesa?" he asked.

CONTINUED, NEXT PAGE...

GROVE CONTINUED, FROM LAST PAGE

"There, Dheb Tyn-Dall."

"I see no one. Where do you say?"

Bheel pointed. "There, Dheb Tyn-Dall, where I point, you see the priestess Lhyreesa taking the late afternoon sun ... unless your eyesight is exceedingly bad, Dheb Tyn-Dall, you cannot fail to see...."

Tyndall's eyesight was exceedingly good. He followed that pointing finger, past the pillar that supported the roof of the patio, past the first row of alien green plants, past the second and third rows, to the clearing, to the little patch of sunlight, to the thing lying there. That monstrous, misshapen Bug.... The Bug.... The Priestess Lhyreesa!

Tyndall felt a pounding, skull-shattering madness closing in on him. This was a joke, of course. No, no joke. A dream then? No, not that either. In only a few split seconds it happened. Tyndall had leapt the rail around the patio, and was streaking through the Grove, heading for its outer boundary. The city—if he could get out of the Grove, there would be places to hide in the city. Narrow streets, empty cellars, dim, dim alleys. They'd never find him there! Run now, run before he was overtaken!

But he was not being pursued. Bheel still stood on the patio, transfixed with horror. He heard the Arrillian's terrified cry "Dheb Tyn-Dall...!" And then a rope shot out and grabbed him by the ankles. Not a rope really, a green something, and there were others around his arms, his chest, his hips, wrapping him in their sticky green embrace. The Guardians! He tried to cry out but one of the verdant fronds enveloped his throat so tightly he could not utter a sound. The innocent green things of the Grove were vigilant guardians indeed. They seemed to be merely holding him immobile, but Tyndall realized with sick horror that their pressure was increasing, so little at a time, but so steadily.

And something was happening out there in the sunlight too. The creature had convulsively grasped the branch of a bush and was clinging weakly to it, great tremors wracking its body. It seemed to be struggling, suffering, dying ... even as he was. In his agony, Tyndall laughed.

"A Time! A Time!" The voice came from the patio. Tyndall saw Bheel throw himself face down on the floor, covering his eyes with his hands. He heard the cry echoed within the palace, and then like a mighty roar outside in the city. And then there was silence, silence broken only by the sound of his own breathing as he dragged his tortured lungs across his shattered ribs.

He saw the Bug give a great heave, and then it seemed to split open, the entire skin splitting in a dozen places and a hand ... A HAND reached from within that dying hulk and grasped the bush to which it clung. A white slender hand on a fragile wrist, and then the arm was free, a woman's arm, a beautiful arm.

"The creature had convulsively grasped the branch of a bush and was clinging weakly to it, great tremors wracking its body. It seemed to be struggling..."

Tyndall began, dimly, and too late, to understand.

A leg kicked free ... the slender ankle ... the amply fleshed thigh.

Tyndall clung to consciousness doggedly. The Guardian was crushing the last dregs of life out of him now, and even the pain seemed to recede. His mind was very, very clear. So that was it. A word once heard in a long forgotten classroom, and then the scientists of the expedition. Metamorphosis ... he had meant to ask them what ... but he remembered now ... what it meant. A passing from one form into another.... Had he failed a biology test once because he didn't know what metamorphosis meant ... dimly ... dimly ... he saw ...

The last thing Tyndall ever saw was the Priestess Lhyreesa as she stepped out of the empty hulk, kicking it away with a disdainful toe. Breathless from her ordeal, she sank to the grass, her breasts heaving with exhaustion.

She sat there for a few minutes in the sunlight, then she tossed her head and spread her long raven hair out on her shoulders, the better to dry it in the waning sun.

THE END

Artwork by Wassily Kandinsky

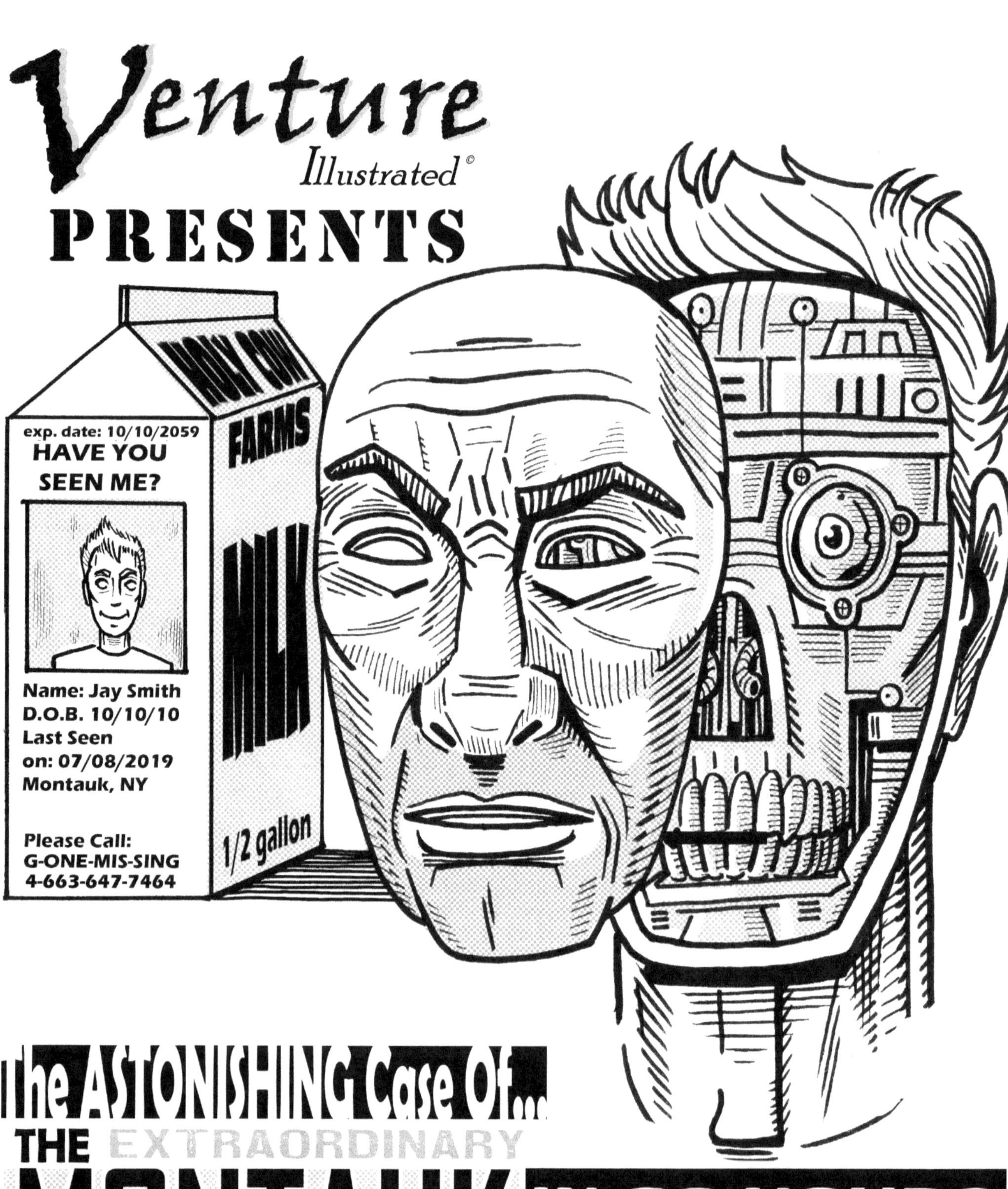

The ASTONISHING Case Of...

THE EXTRAORDINARY MONTAUK MAN

IN 96 HOURS HE BECOMES A THERMONUCLEAR BOMB!

BY YARYAN (WRITER) & FITZ (ARTIST)

NEW AGE brings NEW possibilities. JJ disappeared, then emerged, from shadowy conspiracy. Existence reimagined- his motor skills in OVERDRIVE, no time to speculate the near FUTURE.He fights for SURVIVAL.
The craven, Dispatched, Bleak Agents, persue him...
POP!
POP!

In days past, JJ couldn't FREEFALL or BULLSEYE by the mere light of the moon
Nor FIRE Weapons... such foreign objects
Now his aim is true, SHARP, CONCISE UNEXPECTED state of mind
LIFE HAD PURPOSE

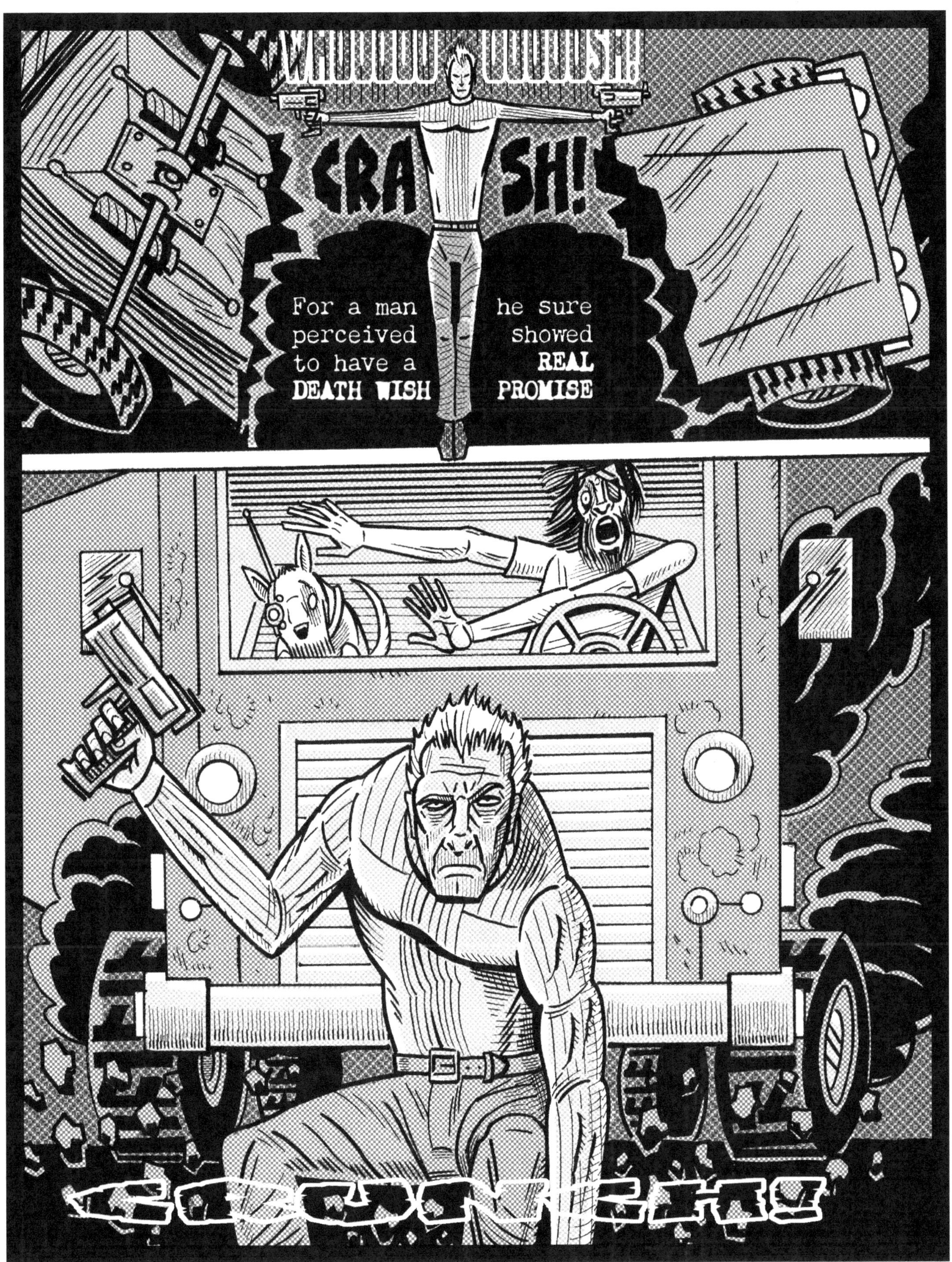
CRA SH!
For a man perceived to have a DEATH WISH
he sure showed REAL PROMISE

SMASH!
For ONCE
in his life
UNBENDABLE
to the wills
of NATURE,
MAN and
MACHINE
CRUNCH!
Convoy stopper--FIRE STARTER
KABOOM!
epicenter of ends,
his smoke signals--
were a BEACON
of DESTRUCTION.
Any ordinary man,
including his
previous being
would be EXPIRED by now
--yet he lives on borrowed time
Many prayers were left UNANSWERED
In the HOLLOW CHAMBERS of his memories
staring DEEP into EMBERS of candlelight
the INEXPLICABLE ascension into
an EXTRAORDINARY CREATION--

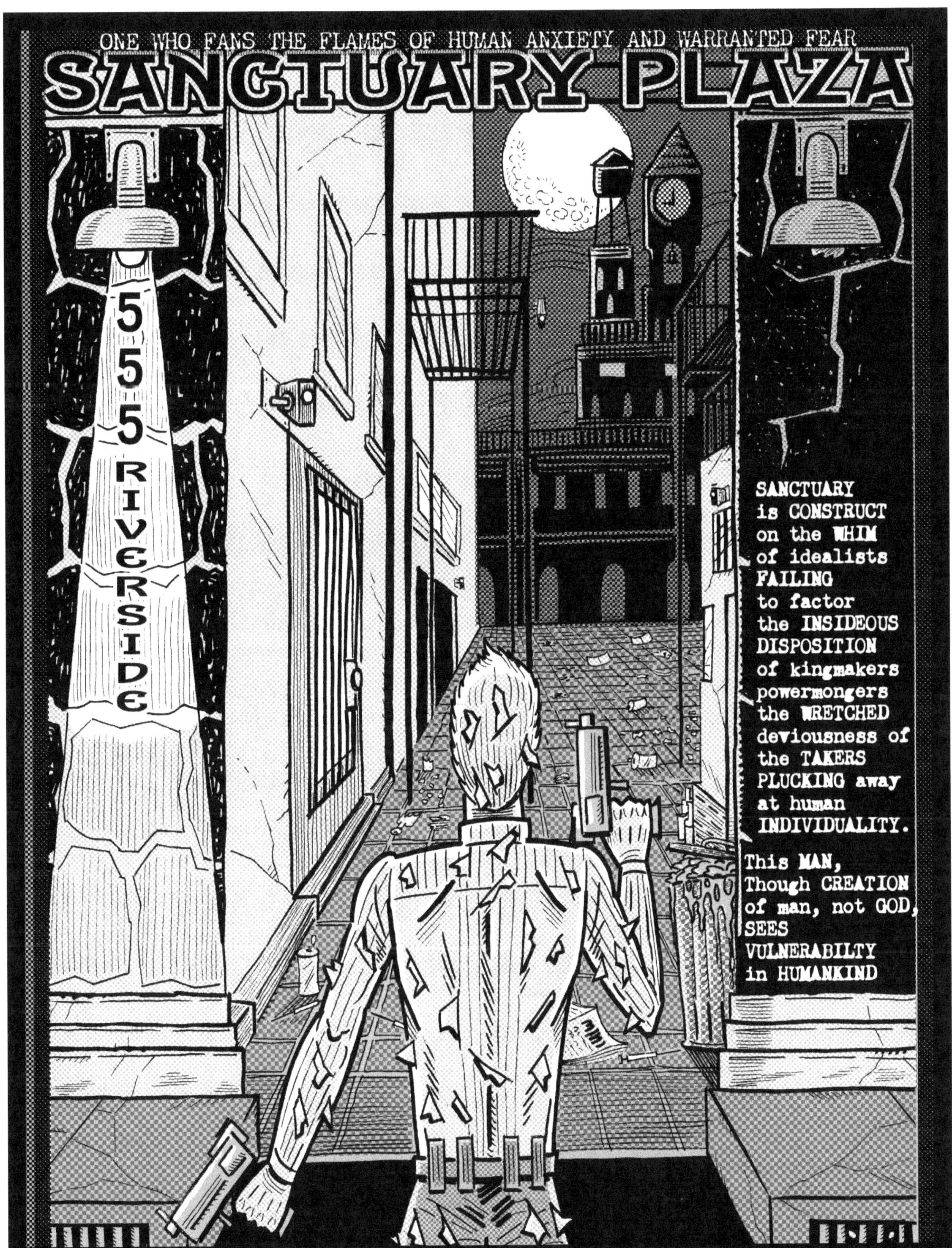
ONE WHO FANS THE FLAMES OF HUMAN ANXIETY AND WARRANTED FEAR
SANCTUARY PLAZA
555 RIVERSIDE
SANCTUARY is CONSTRUCT on the WHIM of idealists FAILING to factor the INSIDEOUS DISPOSITION of kingmakers powermongers the WRETCHED deviousness of the TAKERS PLUCKING away at human INDIVIDUALITY.
This MAN, Though CREATION of man, not GOD, SEES VULNERABILTY in HUMANKIND

The BEASTS
of CERBERUS,
security team,
CTS,
also watch for
the weak spots
They MONITOR
the AFFLUENT BREED
of CONTROLLERS
BEHIND the scenes
Biding TIME
CALIBRATED, in TUNE
to the PULSE
of the instigators
all the COVERT ONES
who've sealed
thier OWN demise
The DEVIL'S
in DETAILS--
watchful eyes
scout
opportune times--

COMPUTING...
4X*2(8.7321-4.003)
2X-Y+7.52*A/B(4)=?
To STRIKE
WITHOUT hesitation
terminate the THREAT

HOLY GLADIATORS, believers in **DEITIES**. Saints **PAINTING IT ALL** rose-colored--daydream deleters, **HARSH** retrievers, all the things that sing in the rain and bury their **BEASTS** in ancestral custom pain-wrecks of mortal plans, pains, beyond bones, the **SCOPE** of training grounds. Raise **YOUR HAND** if you have a **QUESTION** concerning bio-mechanics, **THE APPARATUS:** **SPRINGS**,**STRINGS**, **COILS**, transmitted **MESSAGES**, outgoing, **INCOMING**, adaptor...

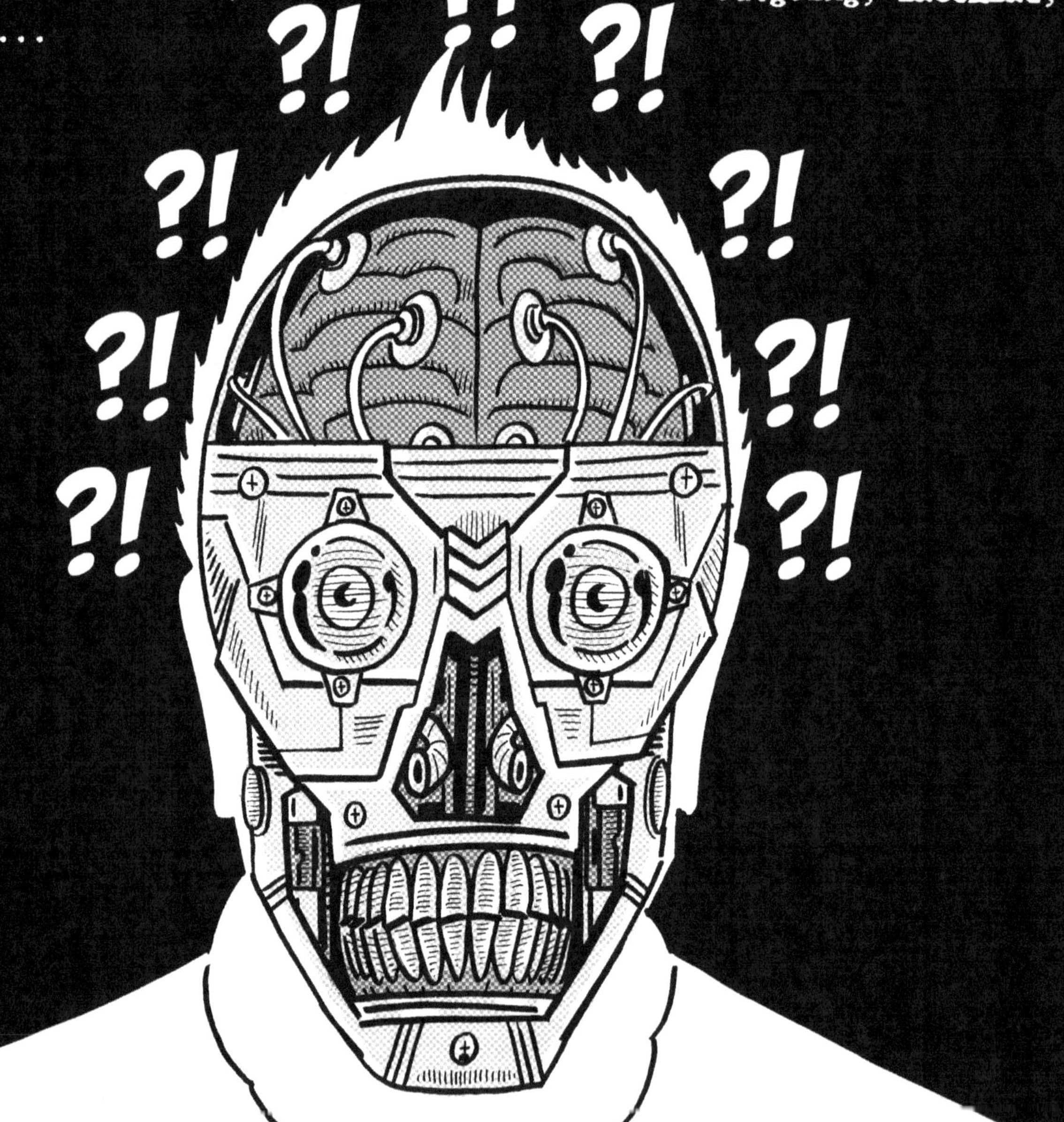

SATALLITE picks up good reception to the exception of the rules. Follow the directions, all signs point to no! Do all **LIFEFORMS** go to heaven after so many **DOG-EARED** tall tale nights, twilights, **HOUNDS OF HELL**--rounding out busy neglect and flights of fancy? Carve the answers in empty caves built by waves of dismay. This may be why man made fire to ward off the **NIGHT-FRIGHTS**...

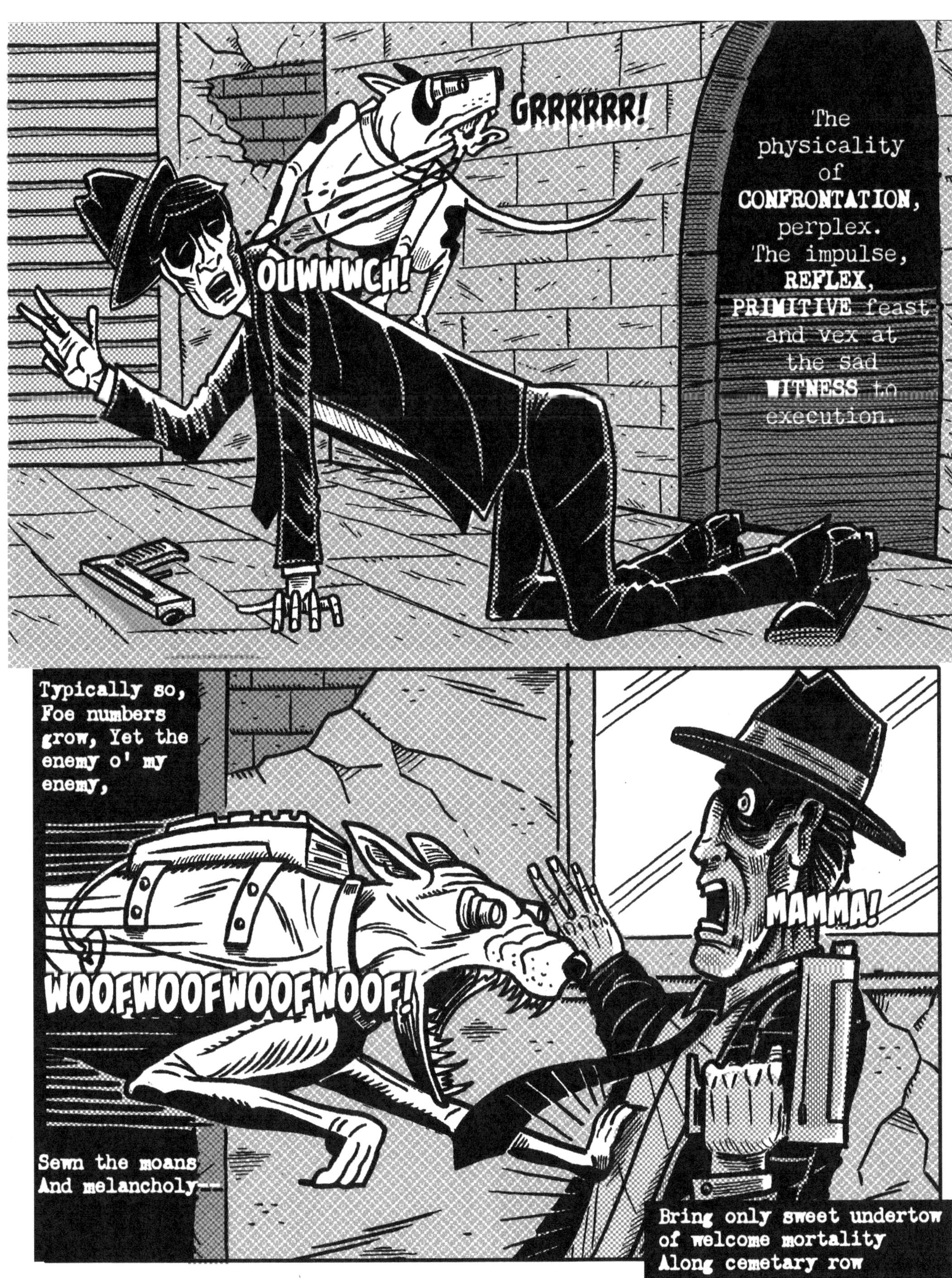
GRRRRRR!
The physicality of CONFRONTATION, perplex. The impulse, REFLEX, PRIMITIVE feast and vex at the sad WITNESS to execution.
OUWWWCH!
Typically so, Foe numbers grow, Yet the enemy o' my enemy,
WOOFWOOFWOOFWOOF!
MAMMA!
Sewn the moans And melancholy--
Bring only sweet undertow of welcome mortality Along cemetary row

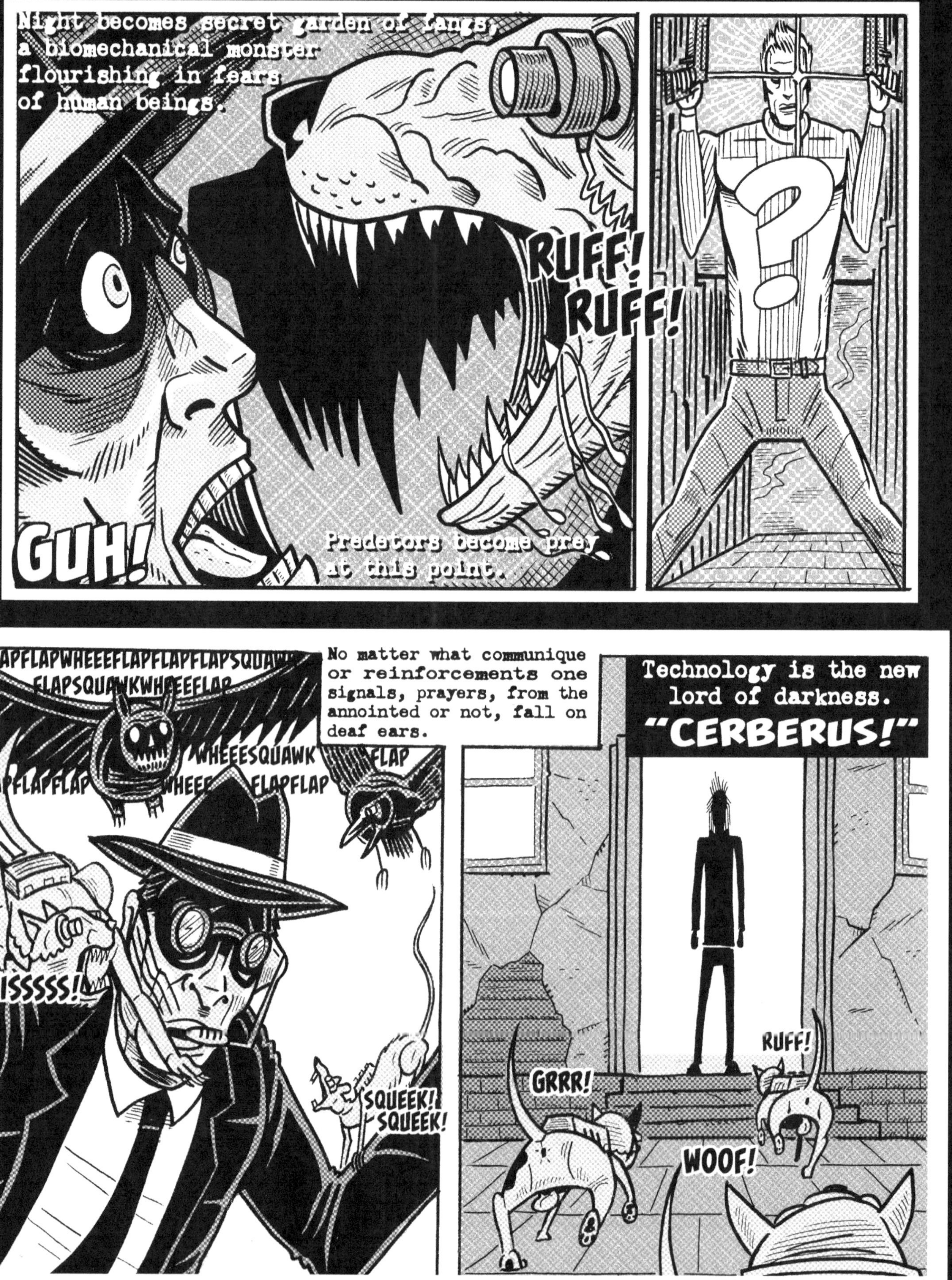

Night becomes secret garden of fangs,
a biomechanical monster
flourishing in fears
of human beings.

RUFF!
RUFF!

GUH!

Predators become prey
at this point.

No matter what communique or reinforcements one signals, prayers, from the annointed or not, fall on deaf ears.

FLAPSQUAWKWHEEEFLAP
WHEEESQUAWK
FLAP
FLAPFLAP
HISSSSS!
SQUEEK!
SQUEEK!

Technology is the new lord of darkness.

"CERBERUS!"

RUFF!
GRRR!
WOOF!

Nothing's shocking anymore, even watching mortal man play God in the dirty alleys of midnight. Miscreants beware, the new age of cybernetic wonder! However, a man made of science should not send his mind on a stroll through theological ambiguities nor mix it up with mortal memories.
Can I be compared to the carnage seekers who've revealed themselves? What has become of me?
The haze of existentialism, the physical horror within, the rapping at the cerebral door, spinal cord battle axe, the doves are taxed and dive into early graves. How must I learn to love the bomb? Ride it out like A rodeo performer cowboy yee-hawing the rocket to RUSSIA! Sometimes, we all need to put catastrophe aside for the greater good of bliss--
and enjoy the convenient TV dinner of life as it was in the atomic age... prior to post-nuclear clarity--

Shadow master calls off the offensive
A.I. creatures adjourn
To the inner-sanctum of their lair
Belonging to their maker,
Known as the REPAIR MAN!
Builder, fixer, proprietor
Forerunner of
new frontier den
of inequity

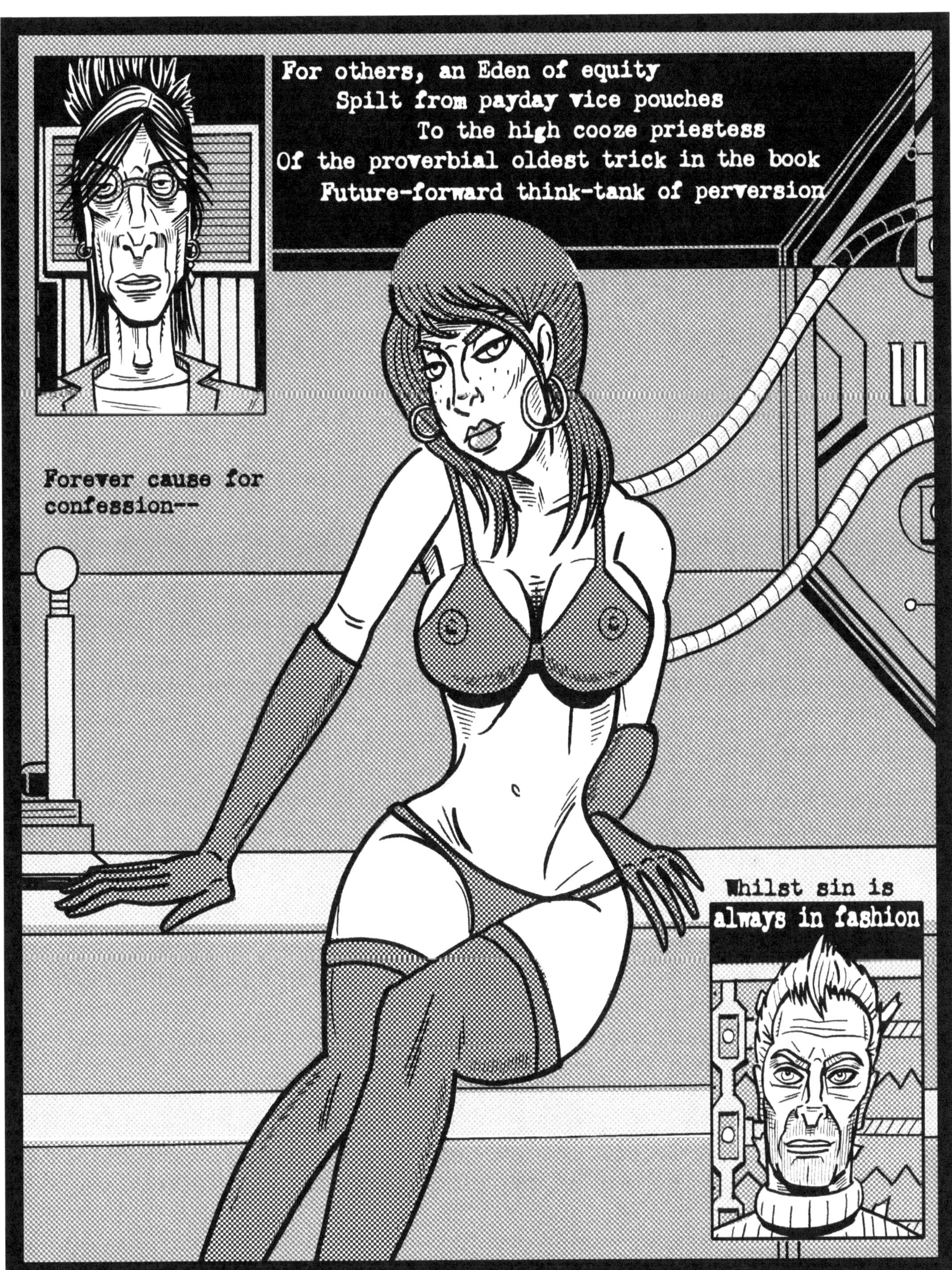
For others, an Eden of equity
Spilt from payday vice pouches
To the high cooze priestess
Of the proverbial oldest trick in the book
Future-forward think-tank of perversion
Forever cause for confession--
Whilst sin is always in fashion

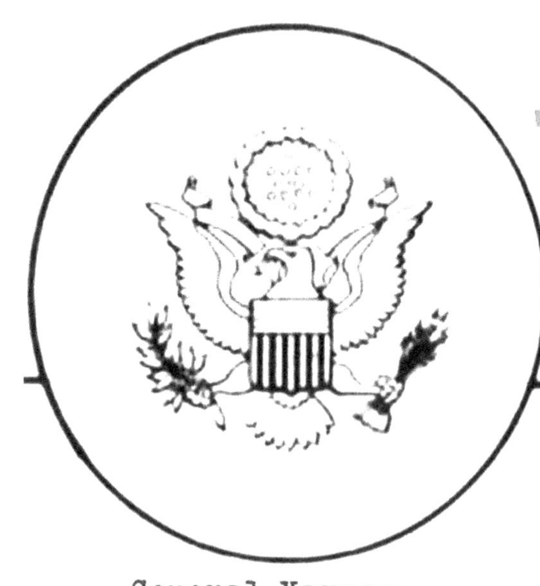

TOP SECRET!

W A R   D E P A R T M E N T
W A S H I N G T O N ,   J U N E   2 ,   1 9 4 3

EYES ONLY!

General Yaryan-

Federal special agents Benjamin T. Sparks and Vanessa C. Winegrove were tipped off exactly one year ago today by an anonymous source, claiming knowledge of an underground compound beneath a church in Provincetown, Massachusetts. The source call was traced to a phone booth in Chattanooga, Tennessee that had subsequently been set on fire post telephone call. The anonymous source's voice recording described alleged heinous experimentation on dead bodies that were buried close to a 150 years ago in unmarked graves that supposedly were unearthed earlier this year by subordinates of Doctor Sylvester Ivan Crinestagger and his partner Doctor Gertrude Greta Richterswil. The source alleged crimes of graverobbing, murder, kidnapping, animal cruelty, necrophilia, torture, undermining the United States Government, unauthorized use of United States Department of Defense equipment, materials and weaponry, illegal covert trade agreements with foreign and domestic enemies, and subversion of government contract resources. The doctors and their accomplices were accused of stripping unmarked graves of Revolutionary War Hessian Soldiers that were buried in proximity to the Old Dutch Church burial ground in Sleepy Hollow, New York. After confirmation of a desecrated graveyard at pinpointed New York location, agents Sparks and Winegrove were prompted to open a case file on Doctors Crinestagger and Richterswil, in addition to their Institute of Superior Science (ISS) based in Baltimore, Maryland. Herewith is documentation of one year of surveillance, discovery and case study evidence of the plot of the ISS and "Operation Hessian."

Colonel Fitz

CLASSIFIED!

Illustration by Fitz

EXTRAORDINARY BOOKS

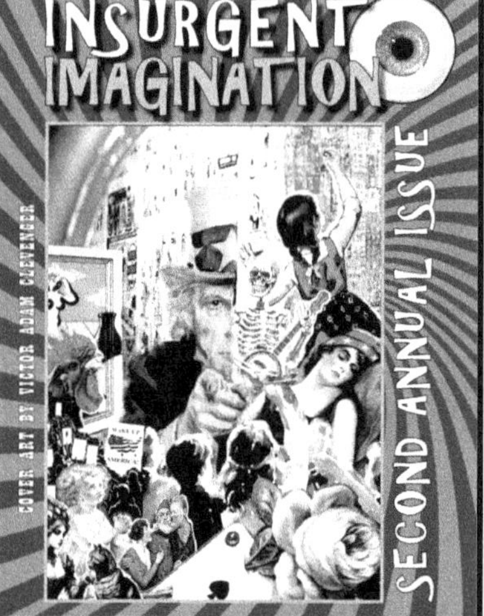

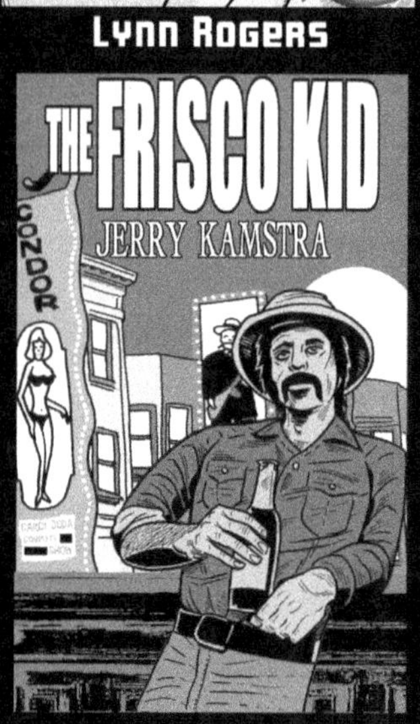

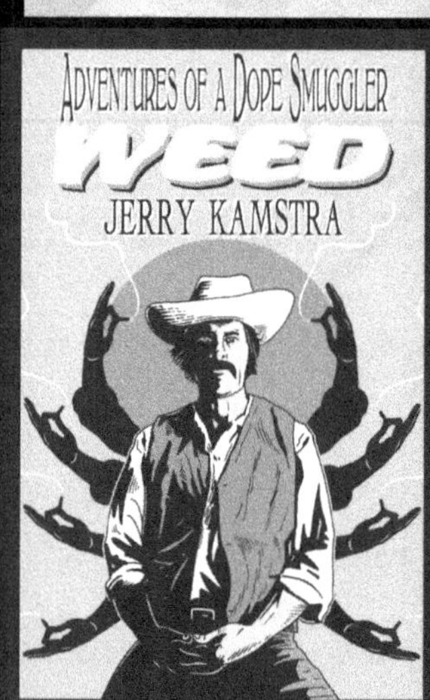

Mystic Boxing Commission

WWW.SPARRINGARTISTS.COM

Sparring With
Beatnik Ghosts
Western U.S. Edition
THE
SPARRING
Artists

www.ingramcontent.com/pod-product-compliance
Lightning Source LLC
LaVergne TN
LVHW081633120826
845149LV00024B/1705

9798993089614